HAPPY BIRTHDAY, SOPHIE HARTLEY

Stephanie Greene

sandpiper

Houghton Mifflin Harcourt
Boston New York

SANDPIPER and the SANDPIPER logo are trademarks of Houghton Mifflin Harcourt Publishing Company.

For information about permission to reproduce selections from this book, write to Permissions, Houghton Mifflin Harcourt Publishing Company, 215 Park Avenue South, New York, New York 10003.

www.hmhbooks.com

The text of this book is set in 13-point Worces Round.

The Library of Congress has cataloged the hardcover edition as follows:
Greene, Stephanie.
Happy birthday, Sophie Hartley / by Stephanie Greene.
p. cm.
Summary: A girl in a large family is looking forward to her first "double digit" birthday, but soon discovers that growing up brings some unwanted changes.
[1. Birthdays—Fiction. 2. Change—Fiction. 3. Brothers and sisters—Fiction. 4. Family life—Fiction.] I. Title.
PZ7.G8434Hap 2010
[Fic]—dc22   2009023346

ISBN: 978-0-547-25128-8 hardcover
ISBN: 978-0-547-55025-1 paperback

Manufactured in the United States of America
DOM 10 9 8 7 6 5 4 3 2 1

4500297041

For Megan Marshall,
the best consultant ever!

⸰ ONE ⸰

On the whole, Sophie felt that the conversation about her birthday present had gone very well.

She'd decided to talk to her father about it first. Sophie liked talking to him about things. He could be more reasonable than her mother. Especially when he was watching TV.

Especially when he was watching football on TV.

Sophie checked to make sure he had a soda and a bowl of chips before she perched lightly on the arm of the couch next to his chair and whispered, "Dad?"

She knew from experience that it was a good idea to whisper her requests. When she whispered, he didn't always answer "What'd your mother say?" the way he did at other times.

"Dad?" she whispered again.

Mr. Hartley leaned his head toward her ever so slightly, keeping his eyes fixed firmly on the screen, and said, "Hmm?"

"You know how I always ask for a dog or a cat for my birthday?" Sophie whispered.

"Hmm?" Mr. Hartley said again. Then he suddenly leaped to his feet, shouted "Go! Go! What are you waiting for, you cowards?" and shook his fist at the TV.

Sophie waited patiently until he settled into his chair again and took a swig of his soda before she went on. "I don't want one this year," she said. "I want a baby gorilla."

If she absolutely had to, she was prepared to add, "It could be my birthday present *and* my Christmas present."

Luckily, she didn't have to make such a rash promise. Mr. Hartley gave a little start, as if Sophie had woken him up from a deep sleep, and cried, "What? Oh, Sophie! Wonderful! Run and get me some more chips, there's a good girl," absently patting her knee as he turned back to the TV.

Sophie hopped up to get the chips. "Wonderful!" he'd said. Her father hardly ever said "Wonderful!" about anything. It was as good as a "Yes" in her book.

It took a bit of practice, but she finally did it.

Hunched over the piece of paper on the floor of the family room, holding her pencil between her big toe and the one next to it, Sophie wrote her name in spidery letters with her foot. Her foot kept cramping from the effort, and she had to stop and massage it several times before she could go on.

It was a good thing gorillas had short names, like Kiki. They were easier to write.

Sophie had fallen in love with gorillas after watching a program on TV about a baby gorilla that was being raised by people in a zoo. It wore diapers and drank from a bottle like a real baby. Sophie thought it looked like a real baby, except much cuter.

She had promptly taken out all the gorilla books she could find from the school's media center. She especially liked the one about the woman who'd moved to Africa to live with gorillas and had died trying to protect them.

Passionate, the book called the woman. Sophie loved that word. Deep in her heart she knew she was passionate. She would be willing to die to protect something she loved, too. Of course, she didn't want to have to do it until she was really old, and she didn't want it to hurt.

But she was definitely passionate.

Another book said gorillas had brains like people and were very smart. At one zoo, a scientist named Dr. Pimm was teaching a baby gorilla how to communicate using sign language.

Because Sophie didn't know sign language, and because all

these animals seemed to do so many things with their feet, she decided to teach herself how to write with her feet, so she could communicate with her gorilla when she got it.

The idea was a little confusing, even to Sophie, but she kept at it. Her mother wouldn't be able to resist when Sophie told her that gorillas didn't scratch furniture or dig holes, and that Sophie was going to be able to write notes to her gorilla telling it what not to do.

She was about to dot the *i* in her name when two arms wrapped themselves around her neck and a high-pitched voice demanded, "Wide! Wide!"

"Not now, Maura," Sophie said. She grabbed her baby sister's hands and tried to pry them from around her neck. Maura promptly lifted her feet off the ground, dangling her entire sixteen-month-old body weight down Sophie's back.

It was Maura's newest trick, and very effective. Sophie could barely breathe.

"Maura, no!" she cried, wrenching her sister's hands apart and dumping her on her bottom. Maura wailed and kicked her heels against the floor.

Sophie ignored her.

It was the only thing to do when Maura had a temper tantrum. She had them a lot these days. Mrs. Hartley said it was because Maura was going through the "terrible twos."

"What do you mean?" Sophie had said. "She's only sixteen months."

"Well then, she's ahead of herself," her mother said. "Gifted. All of my children are gifted."

Sophie personally thought Maura was spoiled. She'd refused to walk for the longest time because so many people in the family were willing to carry her. When Mrs. Hartley made them stop, Maura had started staggering around the house, pulling magazines off tables and books from bookshelves.

Nothing was safe from her grasping hands: pots and pans, dishes on the table, toilet paper, which she delighted in unrolling until all that was left was the cardboard tube. All Mrs. Hartley ever did was say "No, Maura" in a lot nicer voice than she used with everyone else in the family.

For Sophie, the final straw had come the week before. When Maura walked across one of Sophie's wet paintings in her bare feet, Mrs. Hartley had made it sound as if it were Sophie's fault.

"For heaven's sake, work at the kitchen table!" her mother said as she sat Maura on the edge of the sink and held her red, blue, and green feet under the tap.

"But I always paint lying on the floor," Sophie protested. "I think better when I'm on my stomach."

"Well, you'll just have to think sitting up until Maura's older," her mother said. "Honestly, Sophie, use your head."

Sophie was insulted. She went straight up to her room and drew a picture of a baby with a red face, a huge circle for a mouth, a few teeth, and waterfalls of tears gushing out of both eyes. She wrote **DANGER: FLOOD ZONE** under it and taped it to Maura's bedroom door.

She also decided that since it was obvious her mother wasn't going to teach Maura any manners, she'd have to do it herself.

Lesson number one would be patience.

"You can't have everything you want, the minute you want it," Sophie said, crouching over her paper again. "I'll give you a piggyback ride when I'm finished."

Maura stopped kicking the floor and started kicking Sophie's back instead. Sophie scooted sideways on her bottom until she was out of Maura's reach and, using her best teacher-like voice, said, "I'm not going to play with you until you learn patience."

"Patience? Who're you kidding?" Sophie's older sister, Nora, had made her entrance. She tossed her backpack on the couch and made for the family computer. "Number one, you don't know what patience is, Sophie," she said scornfully. "And number two, Maura's still a baby."

As she sat down, Nora frowned at the pencil between Sophie's toes. "What're you doing?" she asked. Then, very quickly, "No. Don't tell me. I don't want to know."

It was too late.

Sophie was so used to Nora's not wanting to hear what she had to say that she took even an idle question as encouragement. If Sophie stopped talking whenever someone in her family wanted her to, she'd never get to explain any of her ideas.

Sophie thought her ideas were interesting.

"One of the biggest differences between primates and Man is that primates don't have thumbs," she explained to her sister's back. "No, wait. Gorillas *do* have thumbs. They even have thumbs on their feet."

Sophie cheerfully bopped herself on the forehead a few times and shook her head to rattle her ideas into their proper place in her brain before she went on. "But they can't write, so scientists are teaching them how to speak."

She cheated a bit by steadying the pencil with her hand as she wrote. "Well, not speak, exactly, but make signs people can read. Sign language, it's called. I thought I'd try to write using my feet to make it equal."

Nora had stopped typing. She was sitting with her fingers poised above the keyboard, staring at Sophie over her shoulder. When Sophie felt her sister's eyes on her, she looked up and smiled.

It was gratifying to think Nora found gorillas as interesting as she did.

"When I get my baby gorilla, I mean," Sophie told her. "For my birthday."

"Do you have any idea how little sense that makes?" At thirteen, Nora had a way of disdainfully curling her mouth whenever Sophie talked, as if Sophie were saying something ridiculous. "Gorillas are learning sign language, so you're going to write with your feet?" she said. "I mean, like, none, Sophie."

Sophie tried to think back to what she'd actually said. She'd been so intent on putting a little smiley face over the *i* in her name that she couldn't remember. It had sounded all right inside her head.

"I don't know why Mom doesn't have you tested," Nora said, sighing heavily as she turned back to the keyboard. "Half the time, the front part of what you say doesn't have anything to do with the end part, and the rest is so insane, none of it makes sense."

"Tested for what?" Sophie said gamely. She found tests interesting. If she didn't always answer the questions the way she was supposed to, it wasn't her fault. Lots of times, there seemed to be more than one answer.

On those horrible end-of-grade tests, Sophie didn't do nearly as well as she thought she should. She blamed the tests.

"I don't know, but there's got to be an explanation." Nora was typing furiously in response to the little boxes popping up all over the computer screen like tiny message bombs. "It's as if you're not dealing with a full deck or something," she said, pecking away.

"Mom said I was gifted," said Sophie. "So there."

"Idiot savant is more like it." Nora typed a bit more, then suddenly jumped as though the seat had shocked her and cried, "Omigod!" in a pleased voice. "I don't believe it!"

"What? One of your *boy*friends again?"

"It's none of your business!" Nora cried, plastering her arms and upper body across the computer screen. "Stop reading my mail!"

It wasn't as if she were holding a pair of binoculars to her eyes, Sophie thought disgustedly. Nora had been acting nuts lately. It was all because she had become boy crazy over the past few months.

She and her friends giggled and shrieked about boys so much, you would have thought they'd never seen one before. Sophie didn't understand why Nora found them so interesting. Especially after living with their brothers, John and Thad.

Boys were—well, boys were either boring or annoying, as far as Sophie could see. The boys in her class walked around flapping their arms with their hands in their armpits to make farting noises. They read joke books, too, then told dumb jokes that nobody laughed at except other boys.

"I don't see why you make such a big deal about boys," Sophie said. "They're exactly the same as girls. You're being sexist."

Sexist was a new word some of the girls in Sophie's class were using. It meant someone who thought boys were better than girls. The girls said boys were sexist. And here was Nora acting sexist herself.

"Right, Sophie. Exactly the same," Nora said. "That shows how much you know, you baby."

Sophie was about to defend herself when Maura grabbed a fistful of Sophie's hair and tried to pull herself to her feet. Sophie yelped and yanked her hair out of her sister's hands, sending Maura onto her bottom again. At that second, their mother appeared in the doorway.

It was Thursday, which meant Mrs. Hartley had started work at 7:30 in the morning, picked Maura up at daycare at 4:00 and dropped her at home, and then gone to pick up John at his tae kwon do class at 4:45. She was always tired by the time she got home on Thursdays.

"Oh, for heaven's sake, Sophie," her mother said. She snatched Maura up before she could utter her first scream and took a quick sniff of Maura's diaper. "You're getting too old to fight with a two-year-old."

"She pulled my hair," Sophie said, rubbing the back of her head.

"That's because you dig in." Her mother glanced at the pencil between Sophie's toes as she turned to leave. "What on earth are you doing?"

"Communicating with apes," Nora told her.

"That, I can believe," said Mrs. Hartley.

· TWO ·

Sophie decided to announce the news at dinner to give everyone plenty of time to think of good gorilla presents for her birthday. She was very glad to hear they were having spaghetti. Everyone in the family loved spaghetti.

When she heard they were having apple pie with vanilla ice cream for dessert, Sophie decided to announce it then. Knowing how good apple pie with vanilla ice cream made her feel, she was sure they'd all be in such generous moods, they'd come up with wonderful present ideas.

She sat all through dinner with a smile on her face, anticipating how excited everyone was going to be when they heard her news.

"There's an awful lot of hammering going on in the garage, Dad," Thad said as he helped himself to seconds. "Can't build a new car out of wood."

"Got a few big birthdays coming up!" said Mr. Hartley, twirling his spaghetti around his fork. "I seem to remember you loved that set of wheels I built for you when you were little."

"Yeah, well, I'm big now," said Thad. "Go-carts don't cut it in high school. I need the real thing."

"Besides," Nora said, "with all due respect, Dad, if Thad drove anything you made, he'd be putting his life in danger."

"You're telling me," John said glumly.

Ever since Mrs. Hartley gave Mr. Hartley a table saw last Christmas, he'd spent most of his spare time in the shop behind the garage. So far, when he wasn't driving his truck somewhere for the moving company, he'd built a bookshelf with crooked shelves, two tables with uneven legs, and a bench for the mudroom.

John had been the only member of the family brave enough to give it a try. It collapsed the minute he sat on it.

Mrs. Hartley immediately went out and bought Mr. Hartley a book on building. He hadn't shown up in the house with any new projects in quite a while. The Hartley children still exchanged nervous looks whenever they heard the whine of the saw.

"Go ahead. Make fun of me," Mr. Hartley said now. "I'm getting the hang of this thing."

"You can make something for *my* birthday, Dad," Sophie said, thinking that even he couldn't ruin a cage.

"Why don't you make something for Maura's room?" Nora suggested as she reached for the last piece of garlic bread. "She can't tell the difference."

"Nice, Nora. Setting up your baby sister," said Thad. He snatched the bread from under her hand.

"Thad! That's mine!"

"Apparently, it's mine."

"Tom . . ." said Mrs. Hartley.

"Right." Mr. Hartley snatched the bread from Thad and ate it himself. "Mmmm," he said. "Delicious."

The flabbergasted silence that followed was too good to pass up. They could celebrate her news over dessert. Sophie opened her mouth to speak, but another voice beat her to it.

"I'm moving up to the attic."

Everyone, including Sophie, looked at Nora.

"I *am*," Nora said. She sat up straight and looked defiantly around the table. "Mom said I could."

"Moving?" Sophie said. "Why?"

"I need my own space."

"Why don't you move to Montana?" said Thad. "I hear there's plenty of space out there."

"But you have your own space," said Sophie. "In our room."

"Exactly."

"I need my own space, too," said John.

"You have your own room, John." Mrs. Hartley pointed to his plate. "Finish your salad or no dessert."

"There's no heat in the attic, is there, Dad?" Thad said hopefully. "Any chance Nora will freeze to death?"

"The room on the left gets some heat through the vent," said Mr. Hartley. "But Thad's right, Nora. It'll be a bit chilly in the winter."

"And a lot hot in the summer," said Thad.

"I'm buying a fan for the summer," Nora told him, "and Mom's getting me an electric blanket for the winter. So there."

"But the attic smells," said Sophie.

The Hartleys' attic was divided into two rooms. A steep and narrow set of stairs led up to a small landing between them. Years earlier, Mrs. Hartley had found Nora and Sophie up there, dividing the mothballs they'd discovered in a garment bag the way they divided their Halloween candy. "They look like candy, but they smell yucky," Sophie had been saying. "You eat one, Sophie, and see what it tastes like," Nora said.

"Off-limits from now on," their mother had told them grimly as she followed them down the stairs. "You'd eat the lavender sachet from my underwear drawer if I didn't keep an eye on you."

"What does lavender taste like?" said Sophie.

Mr. Hartley had put a lock on the attic door that night.

Now here was Nora, moving out of their perfectly good bedroom, a bedroom they'd shared for their entire lives, to live in that smelly place. Not only that, but judging from the look on Nora's face, she could hardly wait.

A person would have to be very eager to have a room of her own to move up to the attic, Sophie thought indignantly. Either that, or desperate to get away from someone.

"I'm not the one who snores," Sophie said.

"Dad snores so loud it makes my Legos rattle," said John.

Mrs. Hartley stood up and started stacking plates. "This isn't about you, Sophie," she said. "This is about Nora being almost fourteen and needing some privacy. You two have done a *wonderful* job of sharing a room all these years. It has nothing to do with you *whatsoever*. Does it, Nora?"

"Of course not," Nora said obediently. She gave Sophie a kind, condescending smile. "If you get lonely, you can come up and visit. Just make sure you knock first."

Knock on her own sister's door? Nora and their mother had obviously been talking about this behind her back for weeks. Happily plotting and planning how Nora could get her own space, far away from her bratty sister, without once asking Sophie how she felt.

No one else in the family seemed to care about how she felt, either.

Mrs. Hartley was telling Mr. Hartley he'd have to set up the bed that had been leaning against the wall of the attic, and telling Thad that she'd need his help in moving the boxes out of the room that was going to be Nora's and into the storage room across the landing.

John was bouncing up and down in his chair, yelling, "I can carry boxes, too! I'm strong!" while Maura shouted, "Me! Me!" as if even she wanted to be a part of it.

"... and the bed a pale, pale blue," Nora said to no one in particular. "I found a picture of exactly what I want in a magazine. I'll go get it."

She jumped up from the table without clearing her plate, which wasn't allowed, but no one stopped her. "I'm going to paint everything else white!" she shouted from the stairs. "The walls, the floor, everything! All white!"

Everyone was acting as if it was such exciting news, and no one was interested in the exciting news Sophie hadn't told them yet. Fine. Sophie stood up and, with great dignity that no one seemed to appreciate, put her plate and glass into the dishwasher and closed it none too gently. If Nora could make her own plans, then so could she. None of them would have anything to do with her gorilla, if that's how they felt.

Especially Nora. Sophie had planned on letting Nora have the fun of feeding it and changing its diapers.

Not anymore.

It would be just the two of them: Sophie and her baby gorilla in their own room. She might even put a sign on the door that said **NO HUMANS ALLOWED.**

"If we all work together on Saturday morning, it won't take any time at all," Mrs. Hartley said briskly as she lifted Maura out of her highchair. "Sophie, if you help, you'll have your new room to yourself by lunchtime."

"Sorry, but I'm busy on Saturday morning," Sophie said, and went straight to the phone to invite herself to Alice's house for a sleepover on Friday.

"I love the color white," Nora said dreamily as she came into their room after her shower. "The whole room white, with carefully selected accents of color." She sighed a contented sigh.

"Hmph," said Sophie.

While Nora was in the bathroom, Sophie had spent the time trying to decide whether she would look emotional or indifferent when Nora said something nostalgic about their last night together in their room.

She was bound to say something. Even Nora would have to say *something.*

But all she did as she pulled back her covers and slid under them was give a little shiver and say, "This room is so frenetic, it gives me a headache."

Sophie didn't know what *frenetic* meant, but it couldn't be very nostalgic if it gave Nora a headache. "Since when?" she said, frowning.

"Since forever."

Sophie got under her covers, too. "Not even you can keep a white floor clean."

"I'm making a 'no shoes' rule." Nora lay flat on her back with her covers folded neatly under her chin. "Everyone has to leave their shoes at the bottom of the stairs."

"You can forget about me visiting, then," Sophie said grumpily. "White's not even a color. My art teacher said white's the absence of color. Who wants to live in a room without color?"

"Not you, that's for sure."

Nora had made no secret of how she felt about the way Sophie mixed reds and purples and oranges and yellows together. And patterns. "Stripes with checks?" she had cried last week when Sophie pulled on her new tights. "Are you nuts?"

"What about your bedspread?" Sophie said. "It has a million colors."

"I know. Unfortunately, I bought it when I was still a child," Nora said, sighing regretfully. "It simply won't fit into my new décor. You can have it when I've saved enough to buy a white one."

Sophie had been admiring Nora's paisley bedspread for months. Now she wouldn't touch it with a ten-foot pole. "No thanks," she said. She turned off her light. "It won't fit into my new décor, either."

"Trust me, Sophie. You don't have a décor."

"I do, too," said Sophie. "I left it in my cubby at school."

Nora's insulting snort was the only thing close to a nostalgic word that either of them uttered on their last night of sharing a room.

· THREE ·

Mrs. Hartley took Maura and John along when she and Nora went shopping for Nora's room the following afternoon. There was nobody to say goodbye to Sophie when she got into Jenna's father's car for the ride to Alice's house.

Sophie was glad she hadn't told Jenna and Alice about it at school. She wanted to do it during their sleepover so they'd have the whole night to make her feel better.

At least she'd get some sympathy from her friends.

She had decided not to tell them about her gorilla until she'd cleared it with her mother. Just in case. At least, that was her plan. But the whole way over to Alice's house, all Jenna talked about was lacrosse.

Lacrosse, lacrosse, lacrosse. It was the only thing Jenna ever talked about since she'd started playing last summer. Sophie was sick of it.

Jenna went on and on for the entire ride like a how-to video. How you had to pass, throw, and *scoop* up the ball! How the stick was called the crosse. How it really hurt when you got hit. How boys were allowed to raise their sticks above their heads but girls weren't, and how girls under the age of ten weren't allowed to check with their sticks.

"That means hit," Jenna explained, even though Sophie was trying to show how bored she was by looking out the window and not talking.

When they got to Alice's house, Jenna was still complaining about how unfair it was to have different rules for girls. She stopped only long enough to say goodbye to her father and go into the house.

While they followed Alice up the stairs, Jenna started bragging about a goal she'd scored at her last game, and Sophie couldn't take it another minute.

"That's not so great," she said. "I'm getting a baby gorilla for my birthday."

"I don't believe you," said Jenna.

"That's not very nice, Jenna," Alice said, closing her bedroom door as the girls dumped their things on the floor. "If Sophie says it's true, it's true."

"I've never heard of a kid having a pet gorilla before," Jenna said.

"So? You haven't heard of everything in the world," said Sophie.

"It's so exciting, Sophie." Alice settled back against the bank of pillows on her bed and smoothed her bedspread out around her. "What are you going to call it?"

"Patsy."

Sophie had been harboring the name in her heart ever since she saw a photograph in one of her books of the tiny, wrinkled face of a newborn gorilla. It looked like a Patsy.

"That's so sweet," Alice said, sighing.

"You can help me take care of it," Sophie told her. "Not *everyone's* going to be allowed to." She gave a meaningful look at Jenna, who was on her hands and knees spreading a comforter over her sleeping bag on the floor between Alice's twin beds.

"I can't believe your mother said yes," Jenna said without looking up. "Your mother never says yes."

"She does, too," said Sophie.

"Not about pets, she doesn't." Jenna sat back on her heels. With her thin face and dark eyebrows, she looked strict. "You've wanted a pet your whole life, and she's never let you."

Jenna was right.

The Hartley children had begged for one kind of pet or another for years. Every time one of them had asked, they'd been met with the same response: "And who's going to *feed* the dog (or newt or guinea pig or cat)?" Mrs. Hartley would say. And before anyone could answer, she'd say, "Me."

There was always a flurry of protest at this remark, and rash promises made, which Mrs. Hartley ignored.

"And who's going to clean its *cage* (or litter box or the messes it made in the yard)?" she'd continue. "Me."

Mr. Hartley was no better.

"What this family doesn't need is another mouth to feed" was all he ever said.

"It's not our fault there are too many of us," Sophie once protested.

"Don't blame me, blame your mother," Mr. Hartley said cheerfully. "I told her we should stop with Thad."

The rest of them had given up. Sophie couldn't. She wanted a pet more than anything. Something warm and soft that she could hold and take care of, that would love her more than anyone else.

Even in a family as big as hers, Sophie sometimes felt as if there was a huge space in her heart that wasn't being used. Something she could call her own might fill it.

But it was one thing for *her* to make it sound as if her mother was unfair and another thing for someone outside her family to do that, so Sophie said, "Well, she did this time, Jenna, so there."

"You two, don't argue," said Alice. "I bet it's because it's Sophie's double-digit birthday."

"The double-digit birthday *is* very important," Jenna grudgingly agreed.

Sophie was the last one of them to turn ten. She'd been hearing about the special birthday presents they got for their tenth birthdays for months. Jenna's parents had sent her to a two-week sleepover lacrosse camp during the summer. Jenna bragged that it was "very expensive."

Alice's mother, who was studying to be an interior decorator, had let Alice buy whatever she wanted for her bedroom. Alice picked pink and green curtains with matching bedspreads and canopies for her twin beds, a round rug covered with pink roses and green leaves, and lots and lots of pillows.

Unfortunately, Sophie didn't think turning ten was going to work nearly as well for her.

For one thing, she wasn't an only child like Alice. And with Maura and Nora, being a girl wasn't as special as it was for Jenna, who had three brothers.

Plus, Mr. and Mrs. Hartley always talked about how expensive it was having to buy presents for two birthdays in a row. Thad's birthday was a week after Sophie's. He was expecting big things this year.

He was turning sixteen.

He'd been bellowing about turning sixteen since the day he turned fifteen.

"Sweet Sixteen!" he'd holler at the drop of a hat. "It's the Big One!"

But it was all too complicated to explain to Jenna and Alice, so Sophie agreed she was probably getting her gorilla because she was turning ten.

"I've still never heard of anyone having one," Jenna said. "Where's it going to sleep?"

Sophie was happy to change the subject. "In my room," she said, turning down the ends of her mouth. "Nora's leaving me."

"What do you mean?" said Alice.

"She's moving up to the attic."

"Great! It's about time!" said Jenna.

"Jenna doesn't mean it's good that Nora's leaving you," Alice said quickly when she saw Sophie's face. "She just means—"

"Yes, I do," Jenna interrupted. "Nora's been bossing you around for years, Sophie."

"You'll love having your own room," Alice told her. "Really."

"Nora tells you what to do all the time," Jenna went on. "You know she does. When you should turn off your light, what to wear every morning..."

"Even how your side of the room should look," Alice said. "Remember when she wouldn't let you use that striped bedspread you found in a garbage bag in front of the thrift shop, because she said it clashed with *her* new bedspread?"

"That was so unfair," Jenna said. She and Alice looked at one another and nodded.

Sophie had been looking back and forth between them as if she were watching a tennis match. "She was worried it had germs," she said when they finally stopped.

They looked at her without commenting.

"I'm used to having her boss me around."

"Then you'll have to get unused to it," Jenna said. Then, suspiciously, "Don't tell me you're afraid of the dark."

"No way!"

"Okay, then."

"You can paint your room whatever color you want, and decorate it and everything!" Alice said in her peacekeeping voice.

"No more bossy Nora telling you what to do," finished Jenna.

It was clear that they didn't understand.

When they were little, Sophie and Nora had fun sharing a room. They made up funny songs and games at night. Sophie was used to the sound of Nora's breathing and the way Nora hummed under her breath when she did her homework.

Sophie felt safer when Nora was in the room. If she admitted that to Jenna and Alice, they'd think she was a baby.

But it was true.

Nora's bed was closer to the closet than Sophie's. Ever since their mother had read them a picture book about a boy with a monster in his closet, Sophie figured that if a monster ever came out of theirs, she could run for help while it was busy attacking Nora. With Nora gone, there would be nothing between *it* and Sophie except air.

Not that she still believed in monsters, of course. There were some nights, though, like after she'd watched a scary movie, when she wasn't sure you could totally rule them out.

Maybe Alice and Jenna were right, Sophie thought resignedly as they went downstairs to make popcorn. Maybe having her own room wouldn't be so bad. She wouldn't mind yellow trim around the windows and pale green walls. And maybe a purple closet door.

Maybe, just maybe, she was going to love her own room when she saw it.

· FOUR ·

She hated it.

From the moment she saw the sad little patches dotting the walls where Nora's posters had been taped, and the bare mattress on Nora's bed, Sophie hated it. It felt as if all the life had been sucked from the room when Nora left.

Sophie didn't even want to go in, it looked so empty. She stood in the doorway beside her mother and said, "Nora took everything."

"I made sure she only took what was hers," Mrs. Hartley said.

Unfortunately, it appeared that almost everything that had made it lively and interesting and homey had been Nora's.

Her bedspread and matching pillows were gone. So were the strings of beads she'd hung from the ceiling around her desk, her desk lamp with the polka dot shade, her cheerleading pompoms, her bulletin board . . . gone, all gone.

The room was an arid wasteland, and Sophie was going to have to live in it, alone, for the rest of her life.

Well, maybe not for the rest of her life, but still.

Nora had taken her desk, too. Four indentations in the carpet showed where it had stood. The empty space was littered with crumpled bits of paper, dust balls, stray paper clips, and an old rubber band.

"Her bed's still here," her mother said with a lot more enthusiasm than the old blanket and lumpy mattress deserved. "Look on the bright side, Sophie! Think of the sleepovers you can have without Nora to disrupt them."

Sophie didn't feel like looking on the bright side. "She even took the curtains," she said. "Everyone can look in."

"Well, she made them." Mrs. Hartley sighed. "Don't worry, we'll get you new ones."

Sophie opened the door to her closet and peered into its depths. "My poor, lonely clothes," she said.

"You did nothing but complain about Nora hogging the entire thing," her mother said with a laugh.

Sophie opened the top drawer of the dresser she and Nora had had to jam their clothing into. "Empty," she said mournfully. She opened every one and slid it shut. "Empty, empty, empty."

"All the more room for you. Really, Sophie. You're so dramatic."

When a wail sounded from downstairs, Mrs. Hartley put her arm around Sophie's shoulders and steered her firmly from the room. "Poor Maura," she said as Sophie followed her down the stairs. "Your father's solution to everything, with all of you, has been to dump you in the playpen."

Mrs. Hartley freed Maura, and they continued to the kitchen. "Let's eat lunch," she said. "I'll tell Nora she needs to vacuum your room before she comes down. She's taken every cleaning tool in the house. We probably won't see her until dinner."

"Good," said Sophie. She wasn't ready to see the new, happy Nora yet. The happy Nora who finally had her own space and didn't miss her horrible little sister one bit.

When they got to the kitchen, Maura began climbing her highchair as if it were a tree. Mrs. Hartley opened a cabinet and took out some glasses. "You know Nora—everything has to be perfect," she said. "Pour some milk in Maura's cup, that's a good girl, and take the plate of sandwiches out of the refrigerator."

"She's not going to let anyone wear shoes in her room," Sophie said.

"Good luck to her," said Mrs. Hartley. "Just think," she went on when they were sitting at the table, with Maura safely tucked in her chair. "You can spread your artwork on your bedroom floor and no one will trample it. With a coat of paint, the room will look brand-new."

"Can I paint it any color I want?"

"I don't know about 'any,'" her mother said evasively. "I seem to remember an argument between you and Nora about purple."

"Nora used to like color. Now she likes everything white. White and clean and perfect."

"She's growing up," said Mrs. Hartley. "Now you don't have to conform to her standards. See? The benefits are already starting."

It was clear her mother's sympathy was fading. "It's so empty," Sophie said, giving it one last try. "A TV would make it feel less lonely."

"I'm glad to see you're feeling better," her mother said. "You'll be amazed at how quickly you can't imagine living without all that wonderful space."

Sophie had already been thinking about space. Specifically, about the empty space where Nora's desk had stood.

"It does feel bigger," she said, trying to sound casual. "There might even be room for a cage."

"Any more talk about cages," her mother said with a pleasant smile, "and I might decide there's enough room for a crib."

"Now, Maura..." Sophie said.

Her mother had run out to the grocery store and asked Sophie to give Maura dessert and wipe her face before letting her out of her highchair. It was too good a teaching opportunity to pass up.

"Would you like a cookie?" Sophie said, waving one back and forth enticingly in front of her sister.

"Mawa cookie," Maura said. She held out her fat little hand.

Sophie sat back. "First you have to say 'please,'" she said primly. "When you want someone to give you something, you say 'please.'"

"Mawa cookie," Maura said, louder this time.

"Say *please*."

"Cookie, cookie, cookie!" Maura shouted, drumming her heels against the chair.

Sophie put the cookie in her lap. "I'm not giving it to you until you ask politely."

Maura continued to squawk, but Sophie refused to budge. All it took was a firm hand and determination. Maybe she'd teach Maura how to tie her shoes after this. Then how to put her dishes in the dishwasher so the rest of them could stop having to clean up after her.

That lesson couldn't come a minute too soon.

It was hard to think with Maura making such a racket, but the more Sophie did, the better her idea seemed. She could train other babies, too, and charge money. Think of all the grateful brothers and sisters who'd be willing to pay.

Of course, if every baby was as noisy as Maura, Sophie would have to invest in a pair of earplugs first. Maura wasn't loud enough, however, to drown out the sound of the mudroom door opening.

Sophie sat forward and thrust the cookie into Maura's hands. Maura stopped yelling immediately.

"Where'd I leave my list?" their mother said as she hurried back into the kitchen. "Oh, there it is." She snatched it off the counter and shook it in the air. "If I end up at the grocery store without this thing one more time, I'm going to scream."

"Maura wanted a cookie, so I gave her one," Sophie told her.

"That was nice of you." Mrs. Hartley smiled at Maura. "What do you say to Sophie, Maura?"

"Pease," Maura said sweetly. "Sank you."

It was mean of her mother, threatening to move Maura's crib into her room just because Sophie had made the slightest suggestion about a pet. Sophie wasn't going to let it stop her. She tore a piece of paper out of her notebook and sat at her desk.

That nice Dr. Pimm who'd raised Kiki in the zoo was sure to write back when she heard how much Sophie loved gorillas and what good care she planned on giving hers.

Her mother would be impressed, too, by how much Sophie

knew about what snack foods gorillas ate and what they did in their spare time. Most important, Dr. Pimm could tell her whether the baby gorilla could sleep in a twin bed without falling out.

Sophie had lifted her mattress to hide the letter until she could mail it, when she stopped. Wait a minute! She didn't have to hide things anymore. It was her own room.

Sophie put it on her desk, in plain sight. This new arrangement might turn out to have its benefits after all. She heard voices on the stairs and quickly sprawled on her bed so whoever it was would see how relaxed she was now that she *finally* had the room to herself.

It was Nora.

She sailed past her old room without as much as a glance in Sophie's direction, laughing and talking with two of her friends who were spending the night so they could practice their cheerleading jumps.

Her friends didn't look at Sophie, either. She heard them dutifully dump their shoes into the wicker basket Nora had put in the hall outside the attic door, then troop up the stairs to the attic. When one of them slammed the door, as if to alert someone who might be listening that they weren't allowed to follow, Sophie sat up.

The nerve of them, slamming the door at her like that!

35
° ° °

"I heard that, Nora!" Sophie shouted. She was used to such rude treatment from Nora, but from total strangers in her own house?

Sophie went downstairs and found the rest of the family watching TV. John and Mr. Hartley were so engrossed in their movie, they didn't even look at her while she complained. Thad said, "Nora who?" before giving her a quick glance and adding, "That's a joke, Sophie. Lighten up."

"You used to complain she paid you too much attention," Mrs. Hartley said, patting the couch next to her. "Sit with us and watch the movie."

Sophie didn't want to watch the movie. If Thad and John and her father liked it, it was all about shooting and explosions. She stomped back up to her room and moved things around for a while to make the room feel more like hers, but it still felt deserted.

She felt a little better after she painted one of the window frames with green and blue and yellow and—too bad for you, Nora!—purple dots. Doing art always made her feel better. She planned on painting the other window frame with different-colored stripes next.

Then, who knew? Animals all over her dresser! The closet door bright yellow! No, more purple! Two coats of purple.

It would serve them right.

Sophie cheered up, thinking about the shocked look that would be on her mother's and Nora's faces when they saw it. Then she started rearranging her belongings and soon felt gloomy again. Her clothes looked limp and lonely in the almost-empty closet. Her underwear slid around in the almost-empty drawer.

There were no two ways about it: her room looked empty. Even with her in it.

Sophie heard faint music over her head, accompanied by laughter and an occasional *thump* when someone jumped. She thought about getting a broom and using the handle to thump on the ceiling, but that would only give Nora the satisfaction of knowing Sophie was paying attention to them.

She finally gave up and got into bed. With the door closed and the lights off, the room felt as huge and empty as a cave. Sophie couldn't sleep with her door open, either, though it might help her feel less lonely. When they came down to use the bathroom, Nora and her friends would think she was a baby.

Between the sounds from the attic and Sophie's active brain, she couldn't fall asleep. She thought about the times when Nora had spent the night at a friend's house, or last summer, when Nora had gone to cheerleading camp for a week.

It had been fun, having the room to herself then. She'd known Nora was coming back.

This time, it was for good.

No more having to yell at Nora to make her turn off her light. No more annoying snuffles from Nora's side of the room when she had a cold. No more Nora saying, "Shut up and go to sleep!" when Sophie talked about one of her interesting ideas.

She was going to be alone for the rest of her life with only a tiny sliver of light under her door for company.

"Good night, Patsy," Sophie said, testing to see how it felt.

Even Patsy ignored her.

Sighing heavily, Sophie rolled over onto her side, her back to the wall so nothing could sneak up on her. Her only cheerful thought came right before she fell asleep.

She'd draw a picture of Nora and write "Unprotected victim in attic" across the bottom and stick it on Nora's door.

Even Nora would have a hard time trying to make a monster take off his shoes before he came up.

· FIVE ·

When Sophie woke up the next morning, she made two decisions: she was not going to show any interest in Nora's room before Nora invited her to see it. Then, as soon as Nora did, Sophie was going to tell her she was too busy.

The trouble was, Nora didn't invite her.

She and her friends listened to music in the attic until lunchtime. Then they walked to the field behind the middle school to practice their cheers. Sophie played a halfhearted game of cards with John in the family room while her parents read the Sunday papers, waiting for Nora to get back.

When she heard Nora in the mudroom, Sophie grabbed a book and threw herself on the couch so Nora would see how busy she was. Nora didn't stop long enough to notice.

She breezed past the family room, called, "Another new poster for my room!" as she waved a poster-size roll happily in the air, and ran upstairs.

"Sophie, why don't you go with her?" said Mrs. Hartley. "You're the only person who hasn't seen her room."

"I'm too busy," said Sophie.

"Reading a book that's upside down must be very time-consuming," Mr. Hartley said.

Sophie took a closer look and threw the book on the table. It was a good thing Nora hadn't noticed.

Her parents were taking Maura and John to the park for ice cream. They invited Sophie to come, but she wanted to stay home and ignore Nora. Besides, Alice had been at the store with her mother when Sophie called earlier to see if Alice wanted to do something.

Sophie was waiting for her to call back.

The longer she waited, the grouchier she got. When the phone finally rang, she ran to it, picked it up, and shouted, "What took you so long?"

There was shocked silence at the other end. Then a voice said, "Is Nora there?"

It was a boy.

A boy for Nora. Sophie couldn't remember a boy ever calling Nora before.

"Hello?" the boy said. "Can I talk to Nora?"

"Nora?" said Sophie.

Another silence. Then, "Isn't this where Nora Hartley lives?"

"Oh. That Nora." Sophie paused to let the boy speak again, but he didn't. "Hold on," she said, and pressed the phone against her stomach.

Nora didn't expect everyone to run up two flights of stairs whenever she got a phone call, did she? Too bad if she did.

"Nora," Sophie said calmly. "Telephone."

She waited for a minute before she spoke into the phone again. "She's not here," she reported.

"Oh." The boy sounded disappointed. "Do you know when she'll be back?"

"Hold on." She pressed the phone into her stomach again and waited. Then she said, "Nope."

"Oh."

This boy sure said "oh" a lot. If this was what talking to a boy on the phone was like, Sophie didn't understand why girls got so excited about it. She stayed unhelpfully silent, waiting to see what he'd say next.

"Well, thanks, anyway," he said, and before Sophie could stop him, he hung up.

"Wait!" she cried, anticipating the expression on Nora's face. "What's your name?"

He was gone.

Sophie put down the phone. Nora would be furious when she found out she'd missed a phone call from a boy. When

Sophie told her she hadn't gotten his name, Nora would be doubly furious.

As it turned out, Nora was so excited it had been a boy, she wasn't mad at all.

"A boy? Really?" she said when she came downstairs. "Why didn't you call me?"

"I did," said Sophie. "You didn't hear me."

"I was listening to music," Nora said, tossing her hair back over her shoulder. "What'd he sound like?"

"A boy."

"What kind of boy?" Nora got a dreamy look on her face. "Like maybe he has shiny dark brown hair that's almost down to his shoulders, and really, really blue eyes? And maybe he plays the saxophone in the school band?"

Wow. She was in worse shape than Sophie had realized.

"Never mind," Nora said before Sophie could answer. She picked up the phone and began stabbing the buttons. "Wait until Leslie hears. And don't listen to my phone call. Leslie? I think Ian called me. No . . . my little sister answered the phone."

"I'm not that little," said Sophie.

"No . . . I was in my room. You know I don't." Nora was drifting toward the stairs. "We're probably the only family in America that doesn't have cell phones. They should do a documentary on us . . ."

"You're not allowed to take the phone upstairs!" Sophie called.

"You're kidding. They did? They broke up?" A squeal. A pause. "Who dumped who? He did! Good. I do not want to get him on the rebound."

Was he a boy or a basketball? Sophie thought. "If something falls in the toilet and I get my arm stuck trying to get it out, I won't be able to call 911!" she shouted.

It was all in vain. Nora was too far gone to hear or care.

Jenna was standing outside their classroom when Sophie got to school the next morning. Destiny Thatcher was standing next to her. Last year, Sophie, Jenna, and Alice had agreed that Destiny was a snob. This year Destiny and Jenna were on the same lacrosse team. Destiny didn't act snobby to Jenna anymore.

She still did to Sophie and Alice. When she spotted Sophie, Destiny turned and whispered something in Jenna's ear. Then she looked back at Sophie. Destiny's long dark hair was pulled back with a purple ponytail bow that matched her skirt.

Sophie didn't like the look on Destiny's face. Maybe the jeans with the frayed hems and her sneakers with mismatched laces didn't look as cool as Sophie had thought when she put them on that morning.

"Go on," Jenna said, nudging Destiny's side when Sophie stopped in front of them. "Tell her."

"Tell me what?" said Sophie.

"I've never heard of a kid having a gorilla for a pet, either," said Destiny.

"What'd I tell you?" Jenna said.

"We think you're lying," said Destiny.

"Not lying," Jenna said quickly. "Making it up. You know how you are, Sophie."

"Sophie's getting a gorilla?" David Holt, one of the major sound makers in their class, stopped on his way into their room and looked at Sophie with real interest. "Cool."

"A gorilla?" Aaron Mass echoed, coming up behind him. "Holy moly!"

The two boys dropped their packs and started loping around, scratching their armpits and making gorilla noises. Kids passing in the hall laughed.

"Some people are so immature," Destiny said. She flicked her ponytail as if she were flicking it in general. Sophie knew Destiny was flicking it at her.

"Don't look at *me*," Sophie said. "I'm not doing anything."

"All right, everyone, break it up," Mrs. Stearns called as she hurried toward them with an armload of books. "My class, inside, please. Destiny, Aaron, go to your own rooms. The bell has rung."

Sophie liked Mrs. Stearns. She was strict, like her name, but nice. She had been Nora's fourth grade teacher, too. When it was time to write in their journals, Nora had written about the crazy things she and Sophie had done.

The first time Sophie met her, Mrs. Stearns said she felt as if she and Sophie were old friends. It sounded nice, but Sophie had had the uneasy feeling ever since that Mrs. Stearns knew a lot more about her than Sophie would have liked.

"Sophie's getting a baby gorilla," David told Mrs. Stearns as they filed in behind her.

"Really?" Mrs. Stearns smiled. "If anyone could, it would be Sophie. Maybe you can bring it to class, Sophie."

"Ohhh, bring it to class, bring it to class," a few girls pleaded, clapping their hands. "I want to hold it." "Baby gorillas are so cute."

"Sophie can tell us all about it when she gets it," said Mrs. Stearns. "Right now, it's time for math."

They scattered to put their things away. Sophie was bent over, fishing her math book out of her desk, when a voice said, "In case you didn't know, gorillas are quadrupedal."

It was Brendan Warden.

"What?" Sophie said distractedly. The nerve of Destiny, calling her a liar! Destiny didn't even know her!

"I said," Brendan repeated patiently, "gorillas are quadrupedal, which means they walk on all four feet. They also have thumbs on all four."

Brendan was one of the AG kids. Some of the boys called him Mr. Notebook because he carried several notebooks with him at all times. He had a different color notebook for each subject. No matter what he was talking about, he sounded like a tour guide in a museum.

"I already know that," Sophie said.

"I'll continue to feed you information as I get it," Brendan said.

"Fine." Sophie slapped her book on her desk. And for Destiny to call herself and Jenna "we"?

"We" had been Sophie, Alice, and Jenna since the first grade. Why hadn't Jenna corrected her?

"Don't worry," Alice said on the bus on the way home. "Destiny always makes friends with someone and then tries to turn them against their other friends. Jenna won't let her."

"I wouldn't be too sure of that," Sophie said.

"Why?"

"Jenna's growing a ponytail."

"No way!"

Sophie nodded. "It may not look like a ponytail yet," she said, "but that's what it is." She and Alice looked at each other somberly. Jenna—who had been cutting her hair with nail scissors for as long as they had known her. Sophie told Alice that she had spotted a clip on either side of Jenna's head.

"Clips?" Alice said, as if all hope were lost. "Jenna?"

"Purple clips. They matched Destiny's ponytail bow."

"No."

"Next thing you know," Sophie said, "it'll be a ponytail."

Alice was too shocked to speak. It confirmed Sophie's worst fears.

Sophie was lying on her stomach in her room, drawing, when Nora appeared and stood in the doorway.

"When are you going to come up and see my room?" Nora said.

"I'm busy now," said Sophie. She put down her green pencil and picked up a charcoal gray one. She didn't have to look up to know that Nora was examining her room with ruthless eyes.

"When are you going to do something about decorating your room?" Nora said when her inspection was finished.

"When I want to."

Nora didn't say anything for a minute. Then, "Does Mom know you painted the window?"

"I don't know."

"Other than that, it's pretty depressing."

"I like it this way."

Another silence.

"I can't believe you honestly think you stand a chance of getting a gorilla for your birthday," Nora said. "It's pitiful."

"Don't look!" Sophie shouted. She sprawled flat to cover her drawing of a baby gorilla in diapers lying on a twin bed. "It's none of your business!"

"You're almost ten," Nora said. "Don't you think it's a little *childish* to go around believing you can have things like gorillas?" She made a rude noise in her throat in case Sophie had any doubts. "To say nothing of unrealistic."

"You're almost fourteen," Sophie mimicked, knowing it drove Nora nuts. "Don't you think it's kind of *childish* to go around believing you can make cheerleading when there are a thousand other girls trying out?"

Nora had been practicing her jumps and cheers for weeks. She said she'd given up ballet because she liked cheerleading better, but Sophie thought it was because Nora wanted to be popular when she got to high school.

"That's all you know," Nora said, blushing. "I'm one of the best on our squad."

"What's happening?" said Thad. He stuck his head into

Sophie's room and looked back and forth between them. "Could it be I hear dissension in the ranks?"

"Sophie's so immature, she thinks she's getting a gorilla for her birthday," said Nora.

"And Nora's so immature, she thinks she's going to make cheerleading," said Sophie.

"You're both out to lunch." Thad laughed his superior high school laugh. It always made both Sophie and Nora want to bop him over the head. "You, a cheerleader, Nora? Cheerleaders are babes. And Soph, a gorilla? That's far-out even for you."

"Listen to you," Nora said. "Mr. Authority."

"It's my double-digit birthday, you know," Sophie told him.

"Sorry to have to tell you, little sister, but the only digits worth celebrating are one and six," said Thad. "Besides, gorillas are expensive. Times are tight. You don't want to take money away from my car, do you?"

"Now look who's out to lunch," Nora said. "A car? Get real, Thad."

"Yeah," said Sophie. "We already have a car."

Thad and Nora were immediately united against her.

"Let me impart a bit of big-brotherly knowledge to you," Thad said heavily. "A beat-up van with one hundred and fifty-six thousand miles on it, and a cracker-encrusted car seat in the back, is not a car. Not when you're in high school and very possibly next year's co-captain of the soccer team."

"And not when you're in the eighth grade and being picked up from parties at night," Nora added.

"You don't go to parties at night," Sophie said.

"I will soon."

"Dream on, Nora," Thad said, heading for his room.

"Dream on about your car," Nora called, flouncing off toward the attic stairs.

"Get out of my room, both of you!" Sophie shouted.

It felt good, slamming the door. Now Sophie understood why Nora liked doing it so much.

After dinner John came into her room and they each sat on a bed and tossed a beanbag back and forth. Without Nora telling them to stop, it got boring. Sophie added pillows to the mix to liven it up. She and John started jumping from one bed to the other while trying to catch the pillows and the beanbag in midair. Mrs. Hartley was the one who finally put an end to it.

"Honestly, Sophie," she grumbled as she shooed John out the door. "You're getting too old for this kind of nonsense." She sniffed. "Do I smell feet?"

"How am I supposed to walk without them," Sophie muttered.

"Just look at this mess," her mother said, casting an unhappy eye over the disheveled beds and crumpled pillows on the floor as she left. "Is this how you want to live?"

Sophie firmly shut her door and looked around her room. Very nice, she decided defiantly. Yes, it *was* the way she wanted to live. She might even leave the pillows on the floor and make it look like a harem. Just because Nora wanted her own room to be perfect didn't mean Sophie had to want the same thing.

She could be interested in anything she wanted to, too. Studying animals was a lot more interesting than hitting with something called a crosse or caring whether a boy called you or not.

Feeling free and independent, Sophie went and took a bath.

A group of kids surrounded her at recess the next day.

"Where are you going to get it?" one boy said.

"A zoo."

"What're you going to feed it?" a girl asked.

Sophie had read that mother gorillas chewed up their babies' food for them before spitting it into their mouths. That wasn't passionate, that was disgusting. "It'll drink from a bottle," she said.

"How about bananas?" someone suggested.

Heads nodded. Bananas sounded right for a gorilla.

"What're you going to do with it when it grows up?" said a loud voice. Everyone turned around.

Destiny was standing at the back of the crowd, leaning on her lacrosse stick. Jenna was next to her. She had her lacrosse stick, too.

Sophie frowned. What kind of question was that? No one ever thought about what they were going to do with a pet when it grew up.

"She's going to give it back, of course."

Everyone looked at Brendan.

"Obviously," he said, clutching a blue notebook to his chest, "when you have an animal that's going to be as tall as a grown man and have an arm span of up to eight feet, you have to let it go into the wild or to a zoo."

Good old Mr. Notebook.

"Obviously," Sophie agreed. "You don't think I'm going to keep a three-hundred-pound gorilla in my room, do you?"

Everyone laughed except Destiny.

"Some people will do anything to make friends," Destiny said. She flicked her ponytail. "Come on, Jenna."

Before she followed, Jenna shrugged at Sophie and raised her stick to show that she had to get to practice.

"What did Destiny mean by 'some people will do anything

to make friends'?" Sophie asked Jenna later when they got back to their classroom.

"Don't get mad at me," Jenna said. "I didn't say it."

"You were standing there," Sophie said.

"So? Standing isn't saying."

"It almost is."

"But it's not."

"You two, don't fight," said Alice.

It wasn't her fault that everyone was getting so excited, Sophie thought, dragging her backpack up the driveway. All she'd wanted was a pet.

A warm and cuddly baby gorilla that she could hold in her arms and play with without having it yell "Mine! Mine!" like Maura or tell Sophie how *childish* she was all the time.

This was all Jenna's fault. If she hadn't blabbed to Destiny, no one would be making a big deal about it or expecting Sophie to bring it to school. Now Destiny was dying to prove Sophie was a liar.

If her mother said no now, Sophie would never live it down.

No more putting it off, she decided as she went into the house. She was going talk to her mother about it the second Mrs. Hartley got home from work.

To make sure the conversation went well, Sophie did everything she was supposed to do, and more.

First she finished her homework. Then she made cherry Jell-O with canned fruit cocktail at the bottom, a family favorite.

After that, she set the table. To make it look extra special, she decided to fold the napkins into animal shapes, the way they'd folded paper in art class. She was working on the swan's neck when the mudroom door opened and her mother walked in, carrying Maura.

Sophie came to attention like a soldier standing for inspection. "Wait till you hear the great idea I have," she said.

"Please. No great ideas tonight," her mother said, putting Maura down, sounding tired. "I have to fix dinner, finish writing my reports, and be back at the office in time for a seven-thirty meeting."

"But—"

Sophie was interrupted by the sound of feet pounding down the stairs. "Can Tara and Kate spend the night on Friday?" Nora cried, rushing into the room. "Please, Mom? Cheerleading tryouts are in three weeks, and we haven't decided what to wear to the dance yet! We have so much to talk about!"

"Nora!" Sophie protested. "I was here first!"

"*Please,* Mom?" Nora said.

"It's fine with me." Mrs. Hartley was busy wrestling Maura's arms out of her jacket. "But if there's any more leaping around, rattling the ceiling, your father will make you move back to your old room."

"Anything but that!"

"Is that my perfume?" Mrs. Hartley called after Nora as she ran for the phone.

"Yes! And it's stale!" Nora yelled indignantly.

"No fair," said Sophie. She frowned at Maura, who had dragged her favorite pots and pans out of the cupboard and was banging them together. Even her baby sister got to do what she wanted. "Nora's having another sleepover, and I haven't had one yet."

Her mother was rummaging through the refrigerator. "Why don't you invite Alice and Jenna?" she said. She took out a package of hamburger meat, sniffed it, and put it on the counter along with an onion. "It might inspire you to clean your room."

"Jenna's parents won't let her spend the night anymore until lacrosse season's over," Sophie said. "She has a game almost every weekend. All Jenna talks about is lacrosse."

"Jenna has always liked sports," her mother said, dabbing at her eyes while she chopped the onion. "Invite Alice, then. You two can still have fun."

Nothing was turning out right. Sophie's napkin looked more like an elephant with a swollen trunk than a swan.

She wadded it up and put a fork on it to hold it down. "Jenna said girls who play lacrosse have an easier time getting into a good college," she said.

"It's a bit early to be talking about college," said Mrs. Hartley.

"I'll never get into a good college," Sophie said sulkily.

"I suggest you worry about graduating from elementary school first."

"I don't even *want* to go to college. I'm going to stay here with you and Dad."

"Fine." Mrs. Hartley dumped the onion and meat mixture into a meatloaf pan and patted it down with her hands. "You can take care of us when we're old and grouchy."

"You're already grouchy," said Sophie.

"And with good reason."

The racket Maura was making had reached a high level. Mrs. Hartley slid the loaf pan into the oven and shut the door. "Put Maura in her stroller and take her for a walk to the corner and back," she said. "It'll be good practice for when you have to push Dad and me around in wheelchairs."

"Do I have to?"

"A little fresh air will do you a world of good."

Pushing Maura along the sidewalk did make Sophie feel better. Everything Maura saw delighted her. She reared up in the stroller with her arms outstretched, crying, "Burd, burd," at every robin she spotted in the grass. She laughed at every leaf that spiraled down through the air.

John was in the yard when they got back. He and Sophie raked a pile of leaves; then Sophie dropped Maura into it and jumped in after her. John followed.

When they went inside, disheveled and covered with leaf dust, their mother didn't even yell. She was in a good mood because her office had canceled her meeting. Sophie decided it would be safe to bring up her idea at dinner, after all.

Then, as they were getting ready to sit down, her father came through the door and ruined her plans.

"Bad news about the van," he announced, hanging his jacket on a peg in the mudroom.

The van had been acting up for weeks. That morning, when Mrs. Hartley couldn't get it into reverse at the daycare center, Mr. Hartley had taken it to the garage.

"Is it the clutch?" said Mrs. Hartley.

"I'm afraid so." Mr. Hartley sat down heavily. "You know how expensive that is to replace. Cam said there's no point in doing it on a car as old as this. The transmission's probably going to go next."

"Yes!" Thad cried, thumping the table with his fist.

"Thad, really," said Mrs. Hartley.

"I mean, that's too bad," said Thad.

"I don't think it's too bad." Nora sat down and put her napkin neatly in her lap. "It's the perfect opportunity to buy a decent car for once."

"A decent car we can't afford, you mean," said Mrs. Hartley.

"Yes, well . . ."

Sophie saw her parents exchange an unhappy look. Two birthdays in a row, and now this. It was definitely not the time to say "Does this mean I can't get my baby gorilla?"

· SIX ·

It was fun having just Alice to spend the night. She admired Sophie's window frames and raved about the idea of painting animals on the desk and dresser. She loved the idea of a purple closet door, too.

"You're so daring," she told Sophie admiringly. "My mother would never let me paint anything in my room purple." Sophie didn't mention that her mother hadn't stepped foot in her room since the night she and John had made such a mess of it.

She took out some of her drawings. Alice especially liked the one Sophie had done of a rearing horse in a pasture. The one Thad said looked like roadkill on grass.

"I love it, Sophie," Alice said. "You're like a real artist."

Sophie was so flattered, she offered to draw Alice's picture.

"Can you, really?" Alice immediately sat up straight and folded her hands neatly in her lap. Her parents had a family photograph taken every year for their Christmas card. If there was one thing Alice knew about, it was posing. "How does my hair look?" she asked, smoothing it down.

"Like normal."

Sophie got a book to lean on and a clean sheet of paper. She sat on her bed with her back against the wall and pulled up her knees. "It might not look exactly like you," she warned.

"What will it look like?" said Alice.

"More like what I think of when I think about you," said Sophie. She didn't know why she drew people like this, but she always did. Sometimes people liked it. Other times they didn't. Knowing how easily Alice got hurt feelings, Sophie wanted to make sure she was prepared.

"It'll be all right," Alice said confidently. "You're my best friend."

Sophie certainly hoped Alice would react the way Thad had. He wasn't at all offended that Sophie made his neck and legs look like tree trunks. "The man's all muscle!" he yelled when he saw it.

Mr. Hartley didn't get mad, either, when Sophie drew his picture and showed an open newspaper with a hairy head at the top and two legs sticking out at the bottom.

"Aha!" he'd said, laughing. "You used art to expose my secret to a happy family life, Sophie." He'd even winked.

Nora and her mother had been different.

Nora had immediately torn up the picture Sophie taped to her door on the night Nora and her friends ignored Sophie. She said Sophie had made her look like a scarecrow. "A tacky scarecrow, too," she said. "You might wear an outfit like that, but I never would."

And, "Really, Sophie!" her mother cried when she saw the picture Sophie drew of her. "My nose is not that big!"

"You smell everything," Sophie said. "You know you do."

"That may be so," Mrs. Hartley said, but she didn't look pleased. After Sophie fixed the drawing, her mother said it was "very nice," but Sophie had felt highly insulted when she found it rolled up under the couch a few days later.

Having someone pose willingly for her now was exciting. "Ready?" she asked, looking up to study her subject.

Alice was staring at her. Her face was red. It looked as if she were holding her breath. The minute Sophie looked at her, Alice looked down.

Then she looked back up.

"What?" said Sophie.

Alice looked down again, then up.

Down, up. Down . . .

"What's wrong with you?" Sophie said. "I can't draw your picture if you keep moving your head like that."

"Nothing."

Alice's neck was bright red now. She was the only person Sophie knew whose neck blushed. A boy in their kindergarten class had called Alice "fire engine" one day and made her cry.

Sophie put down her pencil. "If you don't tell me, I won't draw your picture," she said.

Their eyes met and locked. Alice stared for another minute before she took a deep breath and said, "Guess what I got today?"

"What?"

Alice hesitated. Then she whispered, "A bra."

"A *bra?*"

"You don't have to shout," Alice said, looking frantically around the room to check whether anyone had heard.

"But . . . you?" Sophie said from behind the hand she'd clamped over her mouth. "A bra?"

Alice still *looked* the same. The same pale brown hair. The same freckles. Sure, she had a few bumps on her front, but she'd always had a few bumps. They were her stomach. Or weren't they? Could it be they were higher up?

"You don't have to sound so shocked," Alice said stiffly as she folded her arms across her chest. "Don't stare, either."

Sophie clamped her other hand over her eyes.

"And stop acting so ridiculous."

It was hard to tell what she could do that wouldn't make Alice mad. Sophie slowly lowered her hands to her lap, her eyes glued to Alice's face so they wouldn't drift down. "But what do you need one for?" she said cautiously.

"You mean you don't *know?*"

"Of course I *know.* Nora wears one, doesn't she?"

"Oh." Alice sniffed. "So that means you're being insulting."

Sophie knew that sniff. It would ruin their sleepover if Alice stayed hurt. "Sorry," she said quickly.

Alice sniffed her "I forgive you" sniff.

"It's just that Nora didn't get hers until the sixth grade," Sophie said.

"So? There isn't a rule about it." The blush was fading from Alice's neck. "A lot of girls get bras when they're ten. You'll have to get one, too, someday."

"Oh, no. Don't drag me into this," said Sophie. "I'm not getting one until I'm twenty-one."

"Oh, Sophie!" Alice put her hands over her mouth and giggled. "You'll jiggle all around high school if you wait that long."

"Jiggle, jiggle, jiggle," sang Sophie. She tossed her paper and book onto the bed, jumped up, and ran to her dresser. She yanked open her top drawer and took out a pair of socks.

"What're you doing?" Alice said breathlessly.

"You'll see."

Sophie wadded one sock into a ball and stuffed it under her T-shirt. She wadded up the other sock and stuffed it on the other side of her chest. Then, holding her hands against her rib cage to stop the bumps from slipping down, she turned back around and stuck out her chest. "I'm Sophie Hartley," she said. "But you can call me Jiggles."

It was all right after that. Sophie and Alice laughed so hard, Alice finally cried, "I have to pee!" and ran to the bathroom. Sophie put her socks back in her drawer and started to draw.

When Alice got back, Sophie showed her the picture. It was a face with a bright red neck and two huge circles underneath.

"Sophie!" Alice cried. "You're so bad!"

"What'd she do now?" Mr. Hartley asked, sticking his head in the door.

Sophie and Alice shrieked, "Nothing!" Alice frantically shoved the drawing under a pillow, and they sat in front of it, side by side, their guilty faces burning.

"Looks like a pretty exciting nothing to me," Mr. Hartley said before continuing down the hall.

They watched almost a whole movie with Mr. and Mrs. Hartley and John before Alice's neck returned to its normal color and they stopped giggling every time they looked at each other.

Later, when they were in bed with the lights out, Sophie said, "I guarantee you Jenna doesn't have a bra."

"Probably not," said Alice. "All she cares about is shin guards."

"I hope she doesn't try wearing them on her bosom."

"Oh, Sophie!" Alice giggled. "No one says bosom."

"My mother does."

"That's because she's old."

"What does *your* mother call it?"

"Chest."

It was nice having this conversation in the dark. It felt as if they could say anything.

"Let's call it boobs, the way Nora does," said Sophie.

"Boobs sounds so funny."

"Boobs when it's just us, but chest when it's around other people."

"Okay."

And that, pretty much, was that.

Brendan appeared from behind the door to the media center on Monday as Sophie was passing by. He was carrying his blue notebook. He told Sophie he'd cleared "all other irrelevant information" out of it so he could devote it to gorillas.

He'd been popping up at her side like a perky ghost, armed with more gorilla information, at least once a day lately. Sophie wished he'd stop sneaking up on her.

"Did you know that the DNA of a gorilla is ninety-eight percent identical to that of a human?" Brendan said now, glued to her side as they made their way down the hall to their class. He quickly checked a page in his notebook. "Actually, it's closer to ninety-nine percent."

"What does that mean?" Sophie said.

"It means that gorillas are almost exactly like humans."

"Well, of course," she said. "Baby gorillas look like real babies."

"Exactly."

The weird look in Brendan's eyes seemed more demented than passionate. Sophie moved away uneasily and bumped into someone walking behind her.

"What are you two talking about?" Destiny said. "Sophie's pretend gorilla again?"

"I don't know why Destiny keeps sticking her nose in my business," Sophie grumbled to Alice as they stuffed their lunches and packs into their cubbies.

"Don't pay any attention to her," Alice said. "She's had a crush on Brendan since the second grade, when she hit him in the face with her jacket while they were playing tag and made him cry. She's just jealous."

Jenna had come up behind them and was putting her things away. "Why should she be jealous?" she said. "She's our star goalie."

"So? What good is being a star goalie if nobody likes you?" Sophie said.

Jenna stopped. "Speaking of liking, do you like Brendan?"

"He's okay."

"I mean, *like* like." Jenna's voice sounded very unlike Jenna. "You two have been buddy-buddy lately."

"*Like* like?" Sophie said, frowning. "What's that?"

"You know, Sophie." Alice wrapped her arms around herself and rocked back and forth as if she were being hugged.

"Gross!" Sophie cried. "Are you crazy, Jenna?"

When Jenna said "I was just asking," Sophie recognized her new voice. She sounded exactly like Destiny.

Pretending you're not interested in something you're actually dying of curiosity about is very hard work. Sophie was sick of it. Every night when Nora went up to her new room humming contentedly, Sophie wondered desperately what it looked like. It felt as if Nora had moved to a foreign country.

Sophie went upstairs to change her clothes after school. When Nora got home, she decided, she'd casually go up to the attic and tell Nora she wanted to show her something. Maybe she'd say she wanted to talk about Destiny and Jenna. She wouldn't be making that up. Even if Nora said the whole thing was Sophie's fault, it would feel like old times.

The trouble was, Nora's friends were with her again. Sophie sat on her bed and listened to them laugh and talk in the family room. She was beginning to feel as if Nora would never be at home again without being surrounded by her friends.

Friends who were so much more important to her than her own sister that Nora didn't care if Sophie saw her precious bedroom or not.

They were probably on the computer, IMing the friends they'd just talked to on the bus. When Nora shrieked, followed by a group shriek from her friends, Sophie knew they were talking about boys.

That boy Nora liked had probably IMed her or something.

She and Alice and Jenna would never shriek about boys like that, Sophie thought disgustedly. Then she remembered Jenna's ponytail and Alice's bra and was struck by a terrible thought.

What if they all changed? What if everything was so different by the time they got to the eighth grade that they weren't even friends?

Sophie would never become a shrieker. But what if Jenna and Alice did? What if they made a whole group of new, shrieking friends they liked better than they liked Sophie, who was too quiet and didn't shriek?

Destiny would be their leader. Of course. They'd all run around at one another's houses, shrieking and laughing together and having a wonderful time and leaving Sophie out.

Just like Nora.

Oh, no they don't, Sophie thought as she stood up. Not if she could help it. She was tired of being ignored. She, Sophie Hartley, was not going to let people ignore her. Not anymore.

Starting with Nora.

Sophie heard voices on the stairs and looked wildly around her room. There must be something she could do . . .

By the time the girls filed past her door, she was skipping in a circle with her hands held out, singing, "Here we go round the banana bush, the banana bush, the banana bush . . ."

The girls stopped.

"Is that your little sister?" one of them asked.

Ha! Sophie thought. It was working.

"Unfortunately." Nora didn't sound happy.

"What's she doing?" the other girl said, laughing.

"Acting crazy, as usual," Nora said. "Don't pay any attention to her."

Good. Let them think she was crazy. When they got to know Nora better, they'd realize it ran in the family. "Oh, did my baby gorilla fall down?" Sophie crooned, bending down to pick up her imaginary gorilla tenderly. "Upsy-daisy, come to Mama," she said, cradling it in her arms. "That's a good little gorilla."

"Gorilla?" said one girl.

"This I've got to watch," said the other girl.

"We don't have time," Nora said. "Your mothers are going to pick you up in an hour. We haven't figured out a strategy about You-Know-Who yet. Come on."

"Wave bye-bye to the nice people, Patsy," Sophie said as the girls continued down the hall. "Bye-bye, girls."

"I know why you're doing this," Nora said, leaning against the door of Sophie's room after her friends had left.

Sophie kept writing. "Doing what? All I'm doing is my homework."

"You're doing it to annoy me, but it won't work."

"Look who's here, Patsy. It's Aunty Nora," Sophie said. She lovingly stroked Patsy's invisible head. "Wouldn't you like to give Aunty Nora a big kiss?"

"You are so immature," Nora said. "When are you going to start acting your age?"

"Come back, Aunty Nora!" Sophie called to Nora's retreating back. "Patsy wants to give you a kiss!"

Wasn't it immature to keep slamming doors? Sophie

wondered. And why, if it was her age, did people like Destiny and Nora keep telling her how to act? If it was her age, shouldn't Sophie be the one to decide how she acted?

If this was growing up, Sophie didn't want any part of it.

· SEVEN ·

The last period of the day was devoted to writing.

"Get your journals and settle down," Mrs. Stearns called from the front of the room. "Quickly, please. No talking. We're running late."

"There's a problem."

Brendan squatted down next to Sophie in front of the cubbies, his face about two inches from hers, and spoke in a low voice.

"What do you mean?" she asked, leaning away from his tuna-fish breath.

"Gorillas hoot."

"Hoot?" It came out louder than Sophie had intended.

"Brendan and Sophie?" called Mrs. Stearns.

"What do you mean, hoot?" Sophie whispered.

"It's the sound they make," Brendan said. "The sound of a gorilla hooting can carry for a mile in the forest."

"So?"

"So," he said, "if it's going to sleep in your bedroom, what will your parents say when it starts hooting in the middle of the night?"

"Brendan and Sophie!"

Sophie heard giggling as she hurried back to her desk. Brendan and Sophie. How embarrassing.

Darn Mrs. Stearns, Sophie thought as she opened her journal to a clean page and picked up her pencil. She had ears like a bat. No, like satellite dishes.

Two huge, round satellite dishes like the one on the Hartleys' roof. It picked up every channel in the universe. Mrs. Stearns's ears were like that. Except she had two: one on either side of her head.

And those eyes. Those x-ray eyes ...

"Are you writing or drawing?"

Sophie looked up. Mrs. Stearns was looming over her desk, looking down at the exposed pages of Sophie's journal. The expression on her face turned Sophie's blood to ice.

"May I see?"

Before Sophie could think of a way to stop her, Mrs. Stearns reached out and picked up Sophie's journal. Her hand seemed to move in slow motion. Sophie's eyes followed it down ... and up ...

Mrs. Stearns was looking at her journal. Looking ... and

looking . . . and looking. Sophie felt as if she were in a dream, where events were happening whether she wanted them to or not.

"Interesting," said Mrs. Stearns.

Make that a nightmare.

In Sophie's experience, grownups said something was "interesting" only when they didn't like it. Mrs. Stearns flipped to the page before the one Sophie had been working on. She flipped to the page after.

When she finally stopped flipping, she looked at Sophie over the top of her glasses for a second. Then she turned Sophie's journal around so Sophie could admire the face with a huge, round disk on either side and two crossed eyes behind glasses.

This was definitely a case of Sophie's not being sure whether her subject was going to like the picture or hate it.

Sophie prayed that the little wings coming out of the person's shoulders didn't look like bat wings. They could easily be angel's wings, couldn't they? Couldn't someone looking at the picture think Sophie had drawn a creature who saw and heard everything and who was so good and kind, like an angel, that she'd never yell at one of her students?

"Is this supposed to be me?" said Mrs. Stearns.

Sophie knew better than to rush her answer.

From personal experience she knew how easy it was to rush

into a confession only to find that the thing you were confessing to wasn't the thing you were being accused of having done, but a whole different thing. So the minute you confessed, you were guilty of two things. It was amazing how often that happened.

"You?" said Sophie.

"Yes, me." Mrs. Stearns smiled. "You've heard that word before."

Sophie narrowed her eyes and stared at her drawing as if she were giving the question careful consideration. "That depends," she said carefully. "Do you like it?"

Mrs. Stearns looked at it again. "It's very funny."

"Then it's you," said Sophie.

"That was so amazing," Alice said as they ran, giggling, toward the pickup area at the front of the school to wait for Mrs. Hartley. She was taking them to a craft store to buy materials for a class project.

"What did you draw?" said Jenna. "We were all dying to see."

Her mouth dropped open when Sophie told them. Alice's, too.

"I would have died," Alice said, slapping her hand over her heart.

"You? What about me?" said Sophie.

It was the last time she was ever—*ever*—going to draw in

school again. Except possibly in art class. She would never forget the way her heart hammered in her chest as Mrs. Stearns carefully tore out the page, walked back with it to her own desk, put it in her drawer, picked up her book, and started to read.

Without saying another word to Sophie.

"Number nine on the audacity scale," Jenna said, holding up her palm.

"I'm still mad at you," said Sophie.

"Okay. Nine point five," Jenna offered.

It was as much of an apology as Jenna ever made. A nine point five on the scale Jenna's brothers used to keep score of brash moves was the highest compliment she could give.

Sophie slapped her palm.

They were still talking about it when Mrs. Hartley pulled up to the curb in her red rental car.

"Hi, girls," she said as they piled into the back. "How was school?"

Sophie and Jenna and Alice exchanged one highly charged glance and yelled, "Great!" before collapsing in a giggling tangle. Mrs. Hartley was smiling at them indulgently in the rearview mirror when an all-too-familiar voice that seemed to be coming from inside the car made Sophie look up.

Mrs. Stearns was leaning in the front window.

". . . don't think I've seen you since our last conference," Mrs. Stearns was saying.

"That's right," Mrs. Hartley said. "How've you been?"

Sophie sat up. Next to her, Jenna and Alice did, too.

"Just fine." Mrs. Stearns smiled at the three frozen faces in the back seat and then looked at Mrs. Hartley again. "It's quite an experience having Sophie in class."

"Oh, dear," Mrs. Hartley said lightly. "I do hope she's behaving."

"That, she is," said Mrs. Stearns. "In her own Sophie style."

"Oh, dear." Mrs. Hartley's voice wasn't nearly as light.

They were having a parent-teacher conference right in front of her, Sophie thought uneasily, looking back and forth between them. Was that legal?

"She's quite the burgeoning portrait artist," said Mrs. Stearns.

Sophie didn't know burgeoning, but she certainly knew portrait.

So did her mother.

"Oh, dear." Mrs. Hartley's voice sank like a stone.

"It's nothing to worry about," Mrs. Stearns said cheerfully, slapping the car door as she straightened up. "I'm sure that as soon as we can find a way for Sophie to focus her energies, she'll do great things."

There was dead silence in the back seat while Mrs. Hartley pulled away from the curb and into the line of cars leaving the school.

"I'm not even going to ask," she said grimly.

"Good," said Sophie. She ignored the flurry of expressive eye rolling on either side of her and tried to think of something to fill the silence in the car.

Her mother filled it for her. "Oh, I almost forgot," she said, picking up something from the front seat. "I stopped at home on the way here. This came for you."

On the other hand, silence could be good. It certainly would have been preferable to the distinct *thunk* Sophie heard as her heart hit the bottom of her stomach.

Her mother was holding out an envelope for Sophie to take. "How do you know a Dr. Pimm at the Riverside Zoo?" her mother said.

"A zoo?" Alice cried. "Oh, Sophie! I bet it's about Patsy!"

"What are you waiting for?" Jenna said, nudging Sophie's side with a sharp elbow. "Open it."

"Patsy?" Mrs. Hartley said as Sophie reluctantly took the envelope from her. "Who's Patsy?"

NANCY R. PIMM, PH.D., the return label said. Sophie was sorry she'd ever learned how to write. Or that paper had been invented. Or stamps. Or gorillas.

She didn't even want to think about what her mother was going to say.

"Hurry up!" Jenna said, jabbing her again.

"Yes, Sophie," Mrs. Hartley said. "Open it."

Short of opening the car window and hurling the letter out, there was nothing Sophie could do to avoid opening it. "Okay, okay ..." she said. Slowly, she ran her finger under the flap and took out the letter.

"'Dear Sophie,'" she read in a flat voice. This was terrible. She felt like a prisoner being forced to read her own guilty verdict. Her mother was the judge. Jenna was the cruel jailer, sitting beside her, ready and eager to carry out the punishment.

"'I appreciate your fascination with and love of gorillas,'" Sophie read. "'But I don't think you're going to like the news I have for you.'"

She looked at the back of her mother's head.

"Go on," said Alice.

"'Gorillas are at high risk for extinction,'" Sophie read, "'and they are being protected by the countries in which they live. You can no longer buy a gorilla due to the strict laws.'"

What was this? Sophie sat up straighter.

"'Even local zoos have to abide by laws that limit how many gorillas they can have in a collection,'" she read, her voice rising. "'My advice is to adopt a gorilla in a zoo!'"

"Oh, Sophie." Alice's voice was tragic. "Poor you."

"Yes. You'll never get Patsy now, will you?" Jenna said pointedly as she looked at Mrs. Hartley.

Normally Sophie would have glared at Jenna to make her stop. Now she was too busy scanning the rest of the letter. "I can adopt one," she reported excitedly. "I can send money to help pay for its food, and when I go to the zoo, I can visit it!"

She was saved! She couldn't have a gorilla even if her mother said she could!

Her mother.

Sophie looked up to find her mother watching her in the rearview mirror.

"But that means Patsy can't live with you and sleep in your room, the way you planned," Alice was saying.

"It's too bad, don't you think, Mrs. Hartley?" said Jenna. "Sophie can't get a gorilla for her birthday after all."

Here it was. The moment Sophie had been dreading. She held her breath, waiting to hear what her mother was going to say.

It felt as if the car itself were holding its breath. Alice squeezed Sophie's hand in sympathy.

Mrs. Hartley slowly turned into the parking lot in front of the store and parked. She put on the brake and turned off the car. Only then did she turn around. "It certainly is, Jenna," she said. She beamed her false smile at Sophie next. "Too bad, Sophie. I guess this means Dad will have to stop building Patsy's cage."

"Honestly, Sophie."

As her mother pulled away from Alice's house, Sophie sagged back against the seat and took a deep breath. Two times in one day, she'd had to hold her breath while waiting to see what kind of trouble she was in. Make that three times. It had given her a new appreciation for breathing.

"A gorilla," her mother said, shaking her head. "I'm not even going to *ask* how Jenna and Alice got the impression Dad and I were going to buy you one for your birthday."

"I asked Dad . . ."

"I'm sure you did," said Mrs. Hartley. "While he was watching football, no doubt."

Sophie was mentally probing her heart to see if it was broken. Nope. It was in one relieved piece. She felt only a tiny, minuscule bit sad she wasn't getting a gorilla.

Her passion was gone. She might try living without it for a while. It felt so relaxing.

"The things you come up with!" her mother was saying.

"How on *earth* did you think you were going to keep a gorilla in the house? What would it do all day? What were you going to feed it?"

"I thought it might be fun if it ate with us."

"With us?" cried Mrs. Hartley. "At the *table?*" She jerked the car to such an abrupt stop at the red light that in any other circumstances Sophie would have complained of whiplash.

"That's all I need. A gorilla eating at our table. As if Thad and John aren't bad enough." Mrs. Hartley threw up her hands. "Sure, bring a gorilla. While you're at it, why not bring a giraffe, too?"

When her mother started to laugh, so did Sophie. It was such a funny picture: a giraffe bent double at their kitchen table with its neck in knots as it tried to eat, its knees up around its ears.

Her mother finally stopped laughing and wiped her eyes. "What am I going to do with you?" she said. "A gorilla, at your age."

"I don't see what my age has to do with it," Sophie said. "I'm passionate about gorillas."

"You're passionate about everything you happen to be passionate about at the moment," her mother said, starting up as the light changed. "When that passion dies down, you become passionate about something else."

"What's wrong with that?"

"Nothing, except as one's children get older, one hopes that they'll mature," Mrs. Hartley said encouragingly.

"Maturing doesn't mean you have to change everything," Sophie said. "I hope you don't expect me to turn into a totally different person the second I turn ten."

"I should be so lucky."

"Just because someone gets older doesn't mean they have to give up all their good ideas," Sophie went on. The conviction was growing stronger inside her by the minute. "What if I want to be a gorilla scientist someday? I should be doing research about it now."

"No one's suggesting you give up your good ideas," Mrs. Hartley said. "But introducing a touch of realism from time to time—is that too much to ask?" She glanced at Sophie, who was intently reading her letter again, and sighed. "I guess it is."

"Dr. Pimm says I can adopt a wild gorilla that lives in the jungle," Sophie said. "My money will protect the gorilla from poachers. I could even name it after me."

"Now, *that* I can see."

Sophie looked up, the vines of the jungle already thick around her. "You can?"

"Yes," said Mrs. Hartley. "I can't think of a better name for a wild gorilla than Sophie."

° ° °

Mrs. Hartley took Maura upstairs after dinner to put her to bed. When the rest of the family went into the family room to watch TV, Sophie told them about her letter.

"Boo-hoo," Nora said, rubbing her eyes. "No gorilla."

"If Sophie's getting a gorilla, I want an iguana," said John.

"I'm not getting one," Sophie said. "But I might adopt one."

"Trevor's brother has an iguana. It's only this big." John held his hands inches apart.

"Yes, John, but it's going to grow to be this big." Mr. Hartley held his hands as far apart as possible.

"A kid in middle school had shelves for his iguana all over his house," Thad said, settling down at one end of the couch and picking up the remote.

"Dad can build shelves for mine," John said.

"Right. And because they'll be crooked, the iguana can use them like slides," Nora said. "The whole house can become an iguana playground. Right, John?"

"I wouldn't be too sure of that, Nora," Mr. Hartley said. "I think you're all going to be pleasantly surprised to see how much my woodworking skills have improved."

"It would be hard for them to get any worse," muttered Thad.

"I want one! I want one!" John shouted, jumping up and down on the couch.

"Thank you, one and all," Mrs. Hartley said as she came into the room. "John, calm down."

"I'll tell you what, John." Mr. Hartley grabbed John's arm to hold him still. "You can have an iguana when you're twenty-one."

"I can?"

"Absolutely. Your own apartment and your own iguana."

"Dad said I can have an iguana!" John shouted.

"Time for bed," Mrs. Hartley said, holding out her hand.

"It'll serve you right if we all turn into criminals after the devious way you're raising us," Nora told her father as Mrs. Hartley led John down from the couch and out of the room.

"Cool move, Dad," Thad said. "I'll have to remember that one."

"I'm getting an iguana when I'm twenty-one," John sang on his way upstairs. "I'm getting an iguana when I'm twenty-one…"

Sophie went to say good night to her mother and found her reading in bed.

"Thanks for not getting mad at me in front of Alice and Jenna," she said as she scrambled across the covers for a kiss.

"I would never betray a member of my own family," said Mrs. Hartley, kissing Sophie on the cheek. "Jenna was a little too eager."

"I'm not sure Jenna and me can be friends anymore," Sophie said. She leaned against her mother's shoulder. "She's getting to be a snob about lacrosse."

"I wouldn't give up on her too quickly. You two have had your differences before. You're both stubborn."

"That's mostly what we have now—differences," said Sophie. "Differences, then the same. Differences, the same."

"That's what girls tend to do at your age, I'm afraid."

"Do they ever stop?"

"Most of them." Mrs. Hartley patted Sophie's knee. "Something tells me you and Jenna and Alice will be friends for a long time."

It was nice talking about things that were on her mind without having to worry about how she was going to sneak in the subject of a gorilla. Sophie said, "You know what Alice got?"

"What?"

"A bra."

"Oh, my." Her mother sat forward and looked into Sophie's face. "Are you ready for one of those?"

"No way. Absolutely not."

"Fine. Let me know when you are." Her mother settled back against the pillows again. "My advice is, don't rush it. You'll be wearing one for a long time."

"I might never wear one," Sophie said.

"There's always that option."

When her mother sighed, Sophie realized how tired she looked.

"Are you still worried about the car?" Sophie said.

"It's not a very good time to have to buy one."

"You mean because of the important birthdays coming up?" Sophie said helpfully. Other than Thad moaning about a car, she'd noticed that not much was being said about birthdays around the house. Even though she wasn't expecting a gorilla anymore, she didn't want anyone to ignore the subject of presents.

Time was running out.

"We'll manage. We always do." Her mother sounded alarmingly casual. "It's not for you to worry about," she said, kissing Sophie on the forehead. "Go brush your teeth."

It was fine and good to tell her not to worry, Sophie thought as she went into the bathroom. But if she didn't, who was going to? She ticked off potential present givers in her head as she brushed her teeth.

Her mother had made it clear that *she* wasn't worried. As for her father, he could never remember how old any of them were, much less when their birthdays fell. Thad would probably buy her something for his car and then borrow it, and Nora, who Sophie had counted on to buy a real present since she'd started baby-sitting, was so annoyed with Sophie right now, she might not buy anything.

Sophie sighed. All she could be sure of was macaroni glued to something from John and a wet, sloppy kiss from Maura. It wasn't much of a list.

Sophie hated it when her parents worried about money. It made her nervous. And because she loved them and wanted to show them how mature she could be, she decided then and there, foamy mouth and all, that she wouldn't say another word to them about her present.

Not one word, no matter how close her birthday came and not a single person in the family asked her about it or even acted as if they were hiding something.

Sophie went to bed feeling proud and selfless, without any idea of how hard it was going to be to keep her resolve. Especially after Thad got the present of his dreams the very next day, and it wasn't even his birthday.

· EIGHT ·

"Now, this is what I call a car." Thad slowly circled the car his father had just driven into the driveway and ran his hand along the roof. "Six cylinders, power windows, sunroof . . . this, I won't have to drive under cover of darkness."

"No fair," Sophie said. "It's not even Thad's birthday."

"Don't worry," said Mrs. Hartley. "It's not even Thad's car."

Thad was sure acting as if it were. The whole family was admiring it. Sophie didn't understand what the big deal was. The car was tan, like every other car in the world. They'd have to stick a daisy on top of the antenna so they could find it in the mall parking lot.

It wasn't new, either. There was a scratch on one of the rear doors and a small dent on the front bumper. But because Thad was so pleased, Sophie said in a disgruntled voice, "What's so great about it?"

"It's not a van," Nora told her. "And it has a CD player instead of a tape player."

"Raffi was on tape, and you loved him," Sophie said.

"Puh-lease..."

"Leather seats?" Mrs. Hartley said. "Are you sure we can afford it?"

"Relax, honey." Mr. Hartley patted her back reassuringly. "It was a steal."

The car had belonged to a retired navy admiral. Mr. Hartley had moved him into town five years ago and was now moving him to Florida. Mr. Hartley said that it looked as good as it did because it had spent most of the time in the admiral's garage. The admiral was selling it to him "for a song."

"Don't get too excited, Thad," he added. "It has seventy-five thousand miles on it."

"That's almost as much as the van," said Sophie.

"Half, baby, do the math." Thad slid into the driver's seat and wiggled the stick shift back and forth while adjusting the rearview mirror. John got in next to him and went *"Vroom! Vroom!"* and pretended to press the gas pedal.

Even Nora was impressed. She blew on the silver circle on the front of the hood and polished it with her sleeve.

Sophie went back inside to eat breakfast. Who made the rules, anyway? she thought as she poured herself some cereal.

Why was it all right to love a car because it wasn't a van, but if you wanted a gorilla, you were a baby? And what if, now that her parents had used all their money to buy a car, they didn't have any left for her present?

They'd better not try to give her the car for *her* birthday, too, the way they gave the swing set to all the Hartley children for Christmas one year. If they did, and if Sophie was going to keep her promise, she would have to pretend she was happy.

This having to act mature was going to be much harder than she'd anticipated, Sophie realized glumly. And she hadn't even been doing it for a whole day.

She cheered up when she got to school. Alice had already spread the word. Everyone felt sorry for her. Sophie did her best to look sad but brave.

There were several "I'm sorry about your gorilla" cards on her desk when she got to her room. Even Mrs. Stearns was sympathetic.

"We're all disappointed for you, Sophie," she said. "But I have faith in you. Whatever you come up with next will be equally far-fetched."

Brendan sidled up to Sophie when she was standing with Alice at recess. "I was going to inform you that another potential problem is that gorillas sleep starting at six o'clock at night," he said, his finger in his notebook to hold his place, "but I suppose you're no longer interested."

"No longer," said Sophie.

"Fine." Brendan took out his finger and snapped his notebook shut.

"What happened?" Destiny said, stopping next to them as they watched Brendan walk away. "Did you two break up?"

The nerve of her, acting like she was as old as Nora.

"Yep. I dumped him," Sophie said airily. "Come on, Alice."

"You did?" Destiny called after her.

"You can have him on the rebound!" Sophie shouted. She wasn't sure what it meant, but if Nora didn't want a boy on the rebound, she bet Destiny wouldn't, either.

"What did you just say to her?" Alice said excitedly.

"I don't have a clue," said Sophie. If she'd had a ponytail, she would have flicked it.

The best part came when Sophie and Alice were washing their hands in the girls' room on their way back to class. Sophie glanced at Alice as they stood side by side in front of the mirror and said in a low voice, "Are you still wearing that ... that ... *thing?*"

Alice grabbed Sophie's arm with her wet hands and squeezed.

"Ow!" Sophie cried, yanking her arm away. "What was that for?"

"That's how tight it was." Alice's face was fierce. "It cut off my circulation. I'm lucky I didn't die."

"Die from what?" Jenna came out of a stall and stood next to them. Sophie and Alice exchanged a meaningful glance.

"I don't know . . ." Sophie said to Alice. "Do we want to tell one of *them?*"

"I'm not sure," said Alice.

"One of them?" Jenna said, looking back and forth between them in the mirror. "Who's them?"

Sophie and Alice exchanged another heavy look.

"Destiny and those girls," Sophie told her.

"I'm not one of them," said Jenna.

"Then why are you growing a ponytail?"

"Destiny wanted us all to have one because we're a team," Jenna said. "I cut mine off last night, so she's mad at me. I'm sick of her having to be the boss all the time."

Sophie had never seen anything more comforting than the sight of Jenna's familiar, jagged hair. Still, she had to make sure.

"Then who *are* you one of?" Sophie said.

"One of us."

"Us? Who's us?"

It felt as if they were spies, speaking in code. All those

"thems" and "us's" and short sentences meaning complicated things. Sophie wished they could speed it up a bit.

Jenna must have felt the same way. "You and me and Alice!" she said impatiently, making a little circling motion with her hand.

"You mean you like it better when you and me fight and Alice makes us stop?" Sophie said.

"Of course."

"Me, too," said Alice.

"Me, three," said Sophie.

They went out into the hall.

"So what were you talking about?" Jenna said.

Alice told her.

"I hate those things," Jenna said. "I tried on a tank top that had one built into it. I called it the tank top of doom."

Sophie stopped. "You wore one without telling us?"

Jenna stopped, too. "I tried it on in the store for about two minutes. Destiny and some of the other girls were bragging about wearing them."

"You still should have told us."

"I would have, but I wasn't invited to your sleepover. I can't believe you had one without me."

"You can't spend the night during lacrosse."

"You still should have invited me."

"You two, don't fight," Alice said happily. "Tell Jenna about Jiggles, Sophie."

Sophie did.

It got them laughing so hard that the reading specialist came out of her office to find out what the commotion was about and threatened to send them to the principal.

"Can you imagine having to tell Mr. Potter about chests?" Alice whispered, clinging to Sophie and Jenna as they fled down the hall.

"When it's just the three of us, we're going to call them boobs," Sophie told Jenna as they slid into their seats.

That round of hilarity got them raised eyebrows from Mrs. Stearns.

Sophie had vowed she wouldn't say another word to her parents about her present. That didn't mean she couldn't bug her brothers and sisters.

Her birthday was getting closer and closer. So far, Sophie hadn't seen a single important telltale present sign. No shopping bags that people quickly hid when Sophie burst into a room. No bits of wrapping paper hidden at the bottom of the garbage.

Nothing.

"Don't you want to know what I want for my birthday?" she asked Thad, leaning against the door to his room.

"It's taken care of." Thad was on his bed, bobbing his head in time to the music on his headphones. "I got you the prettiest little fuzzy dice for the rearview mirror you've ever seen."

"Very funny," Sophie said.

"Who said I was joking?"

"Nora?"

"Don't talk to me."

"You'll share your toys with me on my birthday, won't you, Maura?" Sophie said, helpfully balancing a block on top of the tower Maura was building.

"Mine!" Maura said, and snatched it back.

The only person in the family who acted as if he might be planning something was John. One day Sophie found him scribbling furiously on a piece of paper when she went past his room. John shrieked and dived under his bed.

Sophie got down on her hands and knees and peered underneath. "What're you making?" she said hopefully. "A surprise for my birthday?"

"None of your beeswax!" John shouted.

He held the paper closer to his chest and inched back against the wall. "It's something for me and Trevor! Go away, you big nosy-body!"

"What do I care?" Sophie said as she got to her feet. "It's probably more war strategy. That's all Trevor and you ever talk about."

"That's all you know," John muttered.

· NINE ·

Mrs. Hartley wasn't in the kitchen when they went down for breakfast on Monday morning. Mr. Hartley had left the day before to move a family to New York. Their mother should have been hustling around the kitchen, yelling at everyone to come down.

Instead, Nora and Sophie discovered her in a miserable heap under the blankets in the middle of her bed.

"Mom?" Sophie said, pushing open the door. "It's seven o'clock."

The heap moaned.

"What's wrong?" Nora asked. She grabbed Sophie by the arms and held her in front of her like a shield as they advanced cautiously into the room. "Tell me you're not sick."

Mrs. Hartley folded back the blanket enough for them to see her damp hair and pale face. "Don't come any closer," she said weakly. She gestured for them to stop, then let her hand flop back onto the blanket. "I'm sick to my stomach, and I don't want any of you to catch it. I think it's a twenty-four-hour bug."

Nora immediately clamped her hand over her nose and mouth.

"It's too late for that," Sophie said. "The family room was probably full of your germs when we played Monopoly last night."

Her mother groaned and pulled the blankets up over her face again.

"You're a big help," Nora said from behind her hand as she grabbed Sophie's arm more tightly and started dragging her toward the door. "I can't get this, do you understand?" Her voice was a furious whisper. "I don't have time to puke for twenty-four hours. I have the dance on Friday night."

"All you think about is yourself," said Sophie.

"We're getting out of here. Do you hear me?"

"Mrs. Dubowski can take Maura to daycare," their mother said feebly. "John will have to miss tae kwon do."

"Right, Mom! Plan B, coming up!" Nora called brightly. They inched slowly into the hall. "You stay in bed until you feel better, you hear me? Don't you dare come out! We'll just keep your nasty old germs right ... in ... there!"

No prison cell door was ever slammed shut more firmly.

If Nora had had a key, she would've locked the door and

swallowed it. Their poor old mother was waiting to throw up again, and all Nora cared about was her dance.

"Shouldn't we at least ask her if she wants some tea?" Sophie said, trailing Nora down the hall.

"Don't open that door!" Nora shouted. She ran down the stairs. "Omigod. If I get sick, I'm going to kill someone!"

"It would serve you right," Sophie said. "Then you'd be sick in jail."

Their mother showed up in the kitchen when they were eating pizza for dinner. The second Maura saw her, she held out her arms and cried, "Mommy! Mommy!"

"Great, Mom. Now look what you've done," Nora said. She covered her mouth and nose with her hand. "Don't you think you should consider the rest of us?"

"I heard a crash," Mrs. Hartley said, pulling her robe more tightly around her.

"John was showing us a new move," Thad said. "Everything's under control."

"What, no salad?" Mrs. Hartley croaked.

"Go back to bed!" Nora said, pointing sternly toward the stairs.

It was a measure of how sick their mother still felt that she obediently turned and shuffled away. Nora got up from the table and opened the door under the sink. She took out a can and began misting the room.

"That's for smells," Sophie protested.

"Smells and germs," Nora said grimly.

"You're ridiculous," Thad said as he pushed back his chair. "If the germs don't kill us, the spray will."

Maura was still fussing in her highchair. "Maura might be coming down with it," Sophie said as she lifted her out. "She's much crankier than usual."

"Take her away!" Nora shouted. She sounded like a queen sentencing someone to the guillotine. "I don't want to breathe the same air!"

Sophie changed Maura's diapers and got her into her pajamas. Then she pulled Maura onto her lap and tried to read her a book. Maura wouldn't sit still. Sophie finally put her in her crib and rubbed her back until she fell asleep.

When she heard her mother's low, soothing voice in Maura's room in the middle of the night, along with Maura's fretful cries, Sophie worried that Maura was sick.

John confirmed it the next morning.

"Maura's got it at both ends!" he reported gleefully, brandishing a peanut butter–covered knife as they all rushed around the kitchen. "Her mouth and her—"

"Spare us, John," Nora ordered. She opened the refrigerator

door and took out a container of yogurt. "We know what 'both ends' means."

"What's with you, Nora?" Thad said as he came out of the mudroom. "You running for president or something? So you throw up for a day. You get to miss school."

"You might not mind getting this thing," Nora said as haughtily as she could with her nose and mouth covered by one of the white masks Mr. Hartley wore in his shop so he wouldn't breathe in sawdust. "*I'm* not going to."

So, of course, she did. On Friday.

"It might be better if you didn't go up there." Mrs. Hartley was on her way out the door to pick up John and Maura when Sophie got home from school. "I had to pick Nora up from school at lunchtime," she said. "She's over the worst of it, I hope, but she's asleep."

"Nora hates to throw up," Sophie said.

"I can't think of many people who like it."

"What about her dance? Can she still go to that?"

"And take the chance of throwing up on her dance partner?" Mrs. Hartley sighed. "No, I'm afraid Nora's down for the count."

Sophie tiptoed upstairs to her room. If Nora was not only sick but missing her dance, too, she'd be in a horrible mood.

Better not to disturb her. Sophie was about to close her door when she heard a faint sound.

She quietly opened the door to the attic and listened.

"Who's there?" called a pitiful voice.

"It's me."

"Would you bring me some water?" Nora's plaintive voice floating down the stairs made Sophie think of a prisoner in a tower.

"Hold on!" Sophie called. She ran down to the kitchen and got a glass of water and carried it carefully up the attic stairs. She was so intent on getting it upstairs without spilling any that she didn't realize she was about to see Nora's room for the first time until she was in it.

It was so Nora.

Everything was neat and tidy, with white walls and floor. There wasn't a single piece of clothing or paper on the floor. Sophie's first thought was that living with her must have been driving Nora crazy.

Her second thought was that having to keep a bedroom as tidy as this would drive *her* crazy.

It was totally Nora's space, from the small rug beside her bed, to the strings of beads that were acting as the closet door, to the small window that was low to the floor because the room was tucked into the eaves and the ceiling slanted.

Sophie could see the tops of the trees in their backyard and clear over the fence into the yard of the house behind theirs. She'd never realized how sunny her own room was until she stood in the cool gray shadow of Nora's.

"Water . . ." Nora moaned from under the covers.

"You have to sit up," Sophie said. She waited while Nora struggled to a sitting position, then handed her the glass. It was a good thing Nora couldn't go to the dance—she looked terrible. Straggly hair hung on either side of her pale face, and there were dark circles under her eyes.

Nobody would have asked her to dance, looking the way she did.

"Do you feel better?" Sophie asked.

"Do I look as if I feel better?" Nora put the glass on her bedside table and slid back under the covers. It gave Sophie the chance to look around.

Through the beaded closet door she saw Nora's shoes lined up in a perfect row on the floor. Her cheerleading pompoms were pinned to the bulletin board over her desk, next to a cluster of photographs.

When Sophie tiptoed over to see who they were, she saw the flyer Nora had pinned there with two bright pink tacks. WOODSIDE MIDDLE SCHOOL BATTLE OF THE BANDS, it read.

The date was today. On it, someone had written, "See you there."

"Ian Forbes is going to be there, and so's Alicia Brooks." Nora had sat up again. "She hates me because I got on the junior varsity squad last year and she didn't. She'll do *anything* to attract a boy she knows I like."

"Was Ian the one who called?" Sophie said.

"The one you almost gave a heart attack to because you yelled at him, you mean."

"He sounded nice," Sophie said. "He'll know Alicia doesn't really like him."

"That's not the way it works. Boys never know anything."

Sophie hoped that Nora's eyes looked as watery as they did because she was sick and not because she was going to cry. It took a lot to make Nora cry.

"You're such an idiot," Nora said, to Sophie's great relief. "Go get me some ginger ale."

The phone was ringing when Sophie got downstairs.

She picked it up and said, "Hello?"

"Hello?" It was a familiar but raspy voice. "Is Nora there?"

"Ian?" Sophie said. "Is that you?"

Ian moaned.

"What's wrong?"

"I'm sick."

"You are?" Sophie said. "That's wonderful!"

Ian moaned again.

"I mean, that's terrible." She was already moving quickly toward the stairs. "Hold on. I'll get Nora."

"That's okay. Just tell her—"

"Tell her yourself!" Sophie cried as she ran down the upstairs hall. "She's right here!" She pressed the phone against her stomach and took the attic stairs two at a time. "Nora!" she said in a loud whisper. "Ian's on the phone!"

"He is?" Nora's wan face peered out from under the blankets. "I can't talk now."

"You have to!" Sophie thrust the phone into Nora's hand. "He's sick, too!"

It was better than any pill. Nora sat up, brushed her straggly hair out of her face, and took the phone.

"Ian?" she said. She mouthed "Get out!" impatiently at Sophie as she waved for her to leave. "Poor you . . ." Nora crooned.

Sophie went contentedly down the stairs. Nora could shriek and laugh with her friends all she wanted. None of them would be willing to put up with Nora's bad moods the way Sophie did.

Friends might come and go, but you could never get rid of

your sister. There was probably a nicer way to put it, but Sophie liked the thought just as it was.

For better or for worse, being a sister was a permanent position.

"Maybe you should sleep in my room tonight," Sophie said. Her mother had sent her up to see if Nora wanted anything for dinner. She didn't. "You'll be closer to the bathroom."

It was very gratifying when Nora agreed.

With one hand on Sophie's shoulder and the other holding her comforter tightly around her neck, Nora staggered down the stairs behind her. "Does Mom know you're doing that?" she said, glancing at the different-colored panels on the closet door. She stumbled across the room and crawled gratefully under the blankets on her old bed without waiting for an answer.

"I painted it that way to see what it would look like," Sophie said. She put Nora's glass on the bedside table. "I may do it all one color instead."

"I like it," Nora mumbled.

"I can paint your door if you want."

"Heaven forbid."

That was the last word she heard from Nora until the middle

of the night. Sophie woke up to the sound of Nora complaining. "You're snoring, Sophie! Roll over on your side," which Sophie obligingly did.

It felt so much like old times, she fell back to sleep at once.

· TEN ·

It was Sophie's birthday. And a Saturday birthday, at that. The best kind.

The first thing she did when she woke up was lie very still and run a mental check of her body to see if she felt any different now that she was ten. Feet...knees...arms...stomach...face. Nope, they all felt the same.

Next, she sat up. It felt a little strange not to have Nora there on her birthday morning. When they were little, whoever woke up first would wake the other one up. For the last few years, though, Nora had been sleeping late. If Sophie dared wake her up, she got mad.

It was kind of nice having no one there to yell at her. There was a small box at the end of her bed. What could it be? Sophie thought happily as she scrambled to pick it up. She hadn't asked for anything, so it could be, well, anything! Something wonderful that she never even knew she wanted but would make her the happiest girl in the world when she got it.

Sophie was very glad to realize that even though she was ten, she wasn't too mature to get excited.

The box made a soft rattling noise when she shook it. Sophie always shook her presents before she unwrapped them. Sometimes she guessed what was inside.

Not this time. When Sophie couldn't bear the suspense for another minute, she tore the paper off. It was a box of crayons.

Crayons? she thought, turning it over and over in her hands. It had to be a trick. Maybe there was a clue inside as to where she should go next to find her *real* present. That was it! It was like a scavenger hunt.

No one would give a person a box of crayons for her double-digit birthday.

Sophie tore open the flap and stared at four rows of brightly colored, pointy tips. They were crayons, all right. If this was what came from being mature, it was definitely more fun being immature.

Sophie felt a distinct weakening of her resolve. She got out of bed and opened her door.

The hall was empty.

That was a good sign. The fact that not even John was hanging around outside the door meant they were all probably waiting in the kitchen to surprise her with her present before they went out for the traditional Hartley family birthday breakfast.

The fact that the kitchen was empty was a bad sign.

Sophie's newfound maturity was rapidly deteriorating. Not even her family, who obviously couldn't care less about her birthday, would go out for her favorite birthday breakfast of pancakes without her, would they?

"Happy birthday, Sophie!" "Oh, where is she?" "Funny, we forgot her. Pass the maple syrup."

"Hello?" Sophie called hopefully as she wandered around the house. "Doesn't anyone want to sing me 'Happy Birthday'?"

She went back upstairs. Muffled voices were coming from behind the closed door of her parents' bedroom. Sophie knocked softly on the door, and the voices stopped.

"Hello?" she said, opening it a crack. "Doesn't anyone want to wish me—"

"Surprise!" Thad jumped out from behind the dresser, John crawled out from under the bed, and Nora threw open the closet door while Mr. and Mrs. Hartley stood happily beaming. "Happy birthday, Sophie!" they all cried.

"I thought everyone forgot," she said.

"Are you joking?" Nora said. "The way you've been wandering around the house with that pitiful face for weeks and weeks?"

"You were driving us raisins!" John shouted, jumping up and down on his parents' bed.

"Driving us nuts, John," said Thad.

"I like raisins!"

"Calm down, John," said Mrs. Hartley. "Happy birthday, Sophie." She came forward with Maura in her arms and gave Sophie a kiss. Maura was holding a balloon.

"Go on, Maura," their mother prompted. "Give the balloon to Sophie and say 'Happy birthday.'"

"Happy birfday, Soapy," Maura said, clutching the balloon tightly to her chest. "Mine."

"That's all right," Sophie said magnanimously. "She can keep it."

"Over here, birthday girl," Mr. Hartley called.

Her father was standing in front of what looked like one of the huge boxes from his moving van. It was covered with a blanket. Sophie's heart started to race when she saw it. Her mother always said that big wasn't necessarily better. But big was definitely more exciting when it was your birthday.

"This is, beyond the shadow of a doubt," Mr. Hartley said, picking up two corners of the blanket like a matador preparing to face down the bull, "my finest effort." Sophie and the rest of the family crowded around. "Ready to be amazed, Sophie?"

"Ready."

"Ta-da!" Mr. Hartley whipped off the blanket to reveal a table. It had delicate dark green legs and a shiny top. The top didn't slant, and the legs weren't crooked. But it was still a table.

Sophie stood with a smile frozen on her face. She knew she couldn't look disappointed. Her father would feel terrible. Since she was ten, she had to act mature. But what was she supposed to do with it?

Then John shouted, "It's an art table!" and Sophie realized that it was the perfect present because she didn't know how much she'd wanted it until it was hers.

"An art table because you're an artist!" John shouted.

"Even more impressive, the legs are even," said Thad.

John was too excited to stand still. "Look at all the things you got with it!" he shouted. Mrs. Hartley had to restrain him from grabbing everything out of the round holders attached along the edges. Sophie went closer to look.

There were eight of them, four on either side. Round containers painted in bright colors. One was filled with colored pencils. The next with lead sketching pencils. There were paintbrushes of different sizes and thicknesses, a set of watercolors, erasers, a ruler, a compass—every container Sophie examined had new and different art supplies in it.

"And this one's for the crayons," Mrs. Hartley said, tapping the only empty container.

Mr. Hartley was running his finger along the two grooves at the top. "These are to keep your pencils and crayons from rolling away," he said proudly. "I made them with a router. And look . . ." He carefully took the edges of a large roll of white paper that was attached to the back and pulled the paper up and forward until it covered the surface of the table. "When you need a clean sheet," he said with a flourish, like a magician performing a trick, "you pull out as much as you need and tear it off."

He neatly tore the piece off and smoothed it out on the table.

"But how did you know?" said Sophie. "I didn't even know."

"You've got to be kidding," Nora said. "Maybe because you've been scribbling on the walls and floors of the entire house since you were about three?"

"And because you're now apparently drawing unflattering pictures of your teacher at school?" said Mrs. Hartley.

"Omigod, Sophie!" Nora said admiringly. "You didn't. Mrs. Stearns?"

"No one has been safe from the Kamikaze Artist," Thad said in a deep announcer's voice. "She strikes without warning and draws insulting pictures when you least expect it!"

"Now, now," said Mr. Hartley. "The birthday girl deserves some immunity."

"Here." Nora thrust a large, flat package into Sophie's hands.

"It's for watercolors. If you don't like it, I'll take it back and get some of the sticky paper I want for my shelves."

It was a pad of paper. Textured, heavyweight paper.

"This is from me." Thad had given her what looked like an apron. It had **ARTIST AT WORK** written on it. Sophie's art teacher had one exactly like it.

"It's an artist's smock, not an apron," he said as she put it on.

"I know." Sophie tied it behind her and smoothed down the front. They were all smiling at her when she looked up. "I really did think everyone forgot," she said with a sniff.

"Fat chance of that," said Thad.

"Oh, no you don't, Sophie," Nora said. "No more crying. You're old enough now to start paying attention to how pitiful it makes you look."

"And no kissing, either!" shouted John, ducking behind his father.

"Give me a hand here, Thad," Mr. Hartley said. He took one side of the table. "Let's take this to Sophie's room."

They all trooped down the hall and into Sophie's room. The table fit perfectly in the spot where Nora's desk had stood. Sophie didn't regret the missing cage one bit.

· ELEVEN ·

Her parents had given her a tall stool for the table. Sophie was working away when her mother called up to her after lunch. "Sophie! The girls are here!"

Sophie could hardly wait to show Jenna and Alice. She closed the cover of her sketchpad and put her pencil in the groove her father had made for it. She moved the ruler to line up with it and then carefully put the crayons she'd let Maura color with this morning into the crayon holder.

Something about her table made her feel neat and precise. Sophie wondered if maybe she'd undergone a personality change because she was ten. Maybe she even looked different.

No. She looked the same. She did look a bit like an artist, though, with that smudge of charcoal on her cheek. Sophie put her face closer to the mirror. And those traces of white and blue in her hair. Maybe she should dab paint in her hair every day. Maybe a bit on her clothes, too.

"Sophie!"

Jenna and Alice were in the kitchen. Sophie's entire family was in the kitchen. Even Thad was there, and he was hardly ever home on the weekends anymore. When Mr. Hartley came in from outside brushing sawdust from his hair, which meant he'd taken a break from his beloved saw, Sophie got suspicious.

It was very strange, the way they were lined up looking at her. Even Jenna and Alice didn't look normal.

"Hi," Sophie said to them. "Come up and see my present."

"First you have to open our present," Alice said.

"Right away," said Jenna.

Jenna looked excited. It made Sophie nervous.

Jenna never looked excited. According to her brothers, it wasn't cool. As for Alice, her face had the same look it had the time she said, "Guess what I got today?"

Sophie checked Alice's neck.

Red.

No. They wouldn't. They would never buy her a bra and expect her to open it here, in front of Thad and her father and everyone.

"Oh, for Pete's sake. It's not going to explode," Jenna said. She lifted up a large cardboard box from the floor behind her and put it on the table. PATSY was written across the top in large blue letters. Sophie relaxed. Unless they'd named the bra, she was safe.

She didn't even have to shake it to know what it was. It was a stuffed gorilla. Jenna and Alice had bought it to make her feel better. "Ohhh, you two . . ." she said.

"Are you going to stare at it or open it?" Nora said.

"Open it!" said Jenna.

"Okay, okay . . ." Sophie jauntily lifted the lid, prepared to act surprised so Jenna and Alice wouldn't be disappointed, and then she froze.

It wasn't a stuffed gorilla.

It was a kitten.

A real live kitten. It was gray and white, and it was curled up tight in a little ball inside a wicker basket, asleep. Sophie saw its stomach moving up and down, up and down.

She almost was afraid to breathe as she reached out with one finger and gently ran it along the kitten's body. It was soft and warm, and the second the kitten felt Sophie, it opened its blue, blue eyes and its sweet pink mouth and yawned.

Then it stretched.

There was a white patch on the tip of one ear.

"Oh, Sophie," Nora breathed. "Pick it up."

Sophie was afraid to pick it up. She knew that the minute

she did, she'd fall in love with it, and that if she fell in love with it and her mother wouldn't let her keep it, she'd die.

She looked from the kitten to Jenna to Alice, and then at her mother, who was smiling at her. Maybe—just maybe—she wasn't going to say "And who's going to *feed* it?" for the first time in Sophie's life. Sophie held her breath.

"What're you waiting for?" said Mr. Hartley. "Pick it up."

Sophie looked at her mother and said, "Can I keep her?"

"I guess you have to," said Mrs. Hartley. "She's yours."

Everyone started talking at once. Sophie gently picked Patsy up and held her against her shoulder as hands reached over and around her to pet the kitten. Patsy was as light as a feather; Sophie's hand easily circled her delicate body.

She tucked Patsy under her chin and looked from Jenna and Alice to her mother again. "But how...,"

"How did Jenna and Alice talk your mean old mother—who has denied you the joy and thrill of owning a pet all these years, when you've wanted one more than anything else in the whole, entire world," said Mrs. Hartley, "and now that you're ten, will take very, very good care of—into letting them give you a kitten?"

"Yes."

"Bullying," said Mrs. Hartley. "Browbeating, whining, pleading, coaxing, threatening..."

"You know how good Jenna is at that," Alice said. "She got the whole thing started."

"I signed the bedition," John shouted. "I signed the bedition!"

"And yes, even a petition," Mrs. Hartley finished up. "Which John signed twenty times."

"And Trevor, too!" shouted John. "And Trevor's brother!"

"And everyone in the family, including your father, and the mailman, and almost every child in your class, Sophie," said Mrs. Hartley. "I must say, when I saw Mrs. Stearns's name, I gave up."

"But how did you do that without my noticing?" Sophie asked Jenna and Alice.

"Easy," Jenna said. "You were busy being buddy-buddy with Brendan."

"Eeuw!" Sophie cried. "*Like* like."

"I should have thought of a petition years ago," said Nora.

"The real deal breaker was," Mrs. Hartley said, "that when I saw what loyal friends Jenna and Alice are, I realized it's because of your big heart, Sophie. Out of all my children, you were the one who could be depended upon to never let a kitten go hungry or begrudge having to clean up after it in any way."

"Nice, Mom. Insult the rest of us, why don't you?" said Thad.

"I still say it was the petition." Nora sat down and held out her hands. "And since I signed it, I get to hold her. Give her to me, Sophie."

They passed Patsy from one person to the other and then put her on the floor. She walked cautiously around, sniffing and reaching out with her paw to touch things. Maura squealed and squatted down, pressing her hand on Patsy's body as if she were trying to make a pancake out of Play-Doh.

"No, Maura, not like that," Sophie said. She sat on the floor beside Maura and gently but firmly held her hand as she guided it lightly along Patsy's back. "Like this," she said. "Gently. Nice Patsy."

"Gently," Maura said obediently. "Nice Patsy."

"No more terrible twos," Sophie said to her mother. "She's getting older."

"Someone certainly is," said Mrs. Hartley.

"I want to take Patsy up and show her our room," said Sophie. She stood up with the kitten in her arms. "Come on," she told Jenna and Alice as she started from the room. "Wait till you see what my father made."

"I want to bring the basket," John said, reaching into the box.

"Maura's coming with you," Mrs. Hartley called.

Even Nora went with them. "I need your help, Jenna," she said. She cozily draped her arm over Jenna's shoulders as they followed Sophie into her room and settled on her bed. "My birthday's not until April, but my mother refuses to even *talk* about a cell phone. I like that petition idea."

John and Maura came into the room and sat on the floor. Sophie put Patsy, asleep, into her basket beside them. "Keep an eye on Maura, John," Sophie said, and sat down at her table.

Nora went on strategizing with Jenna and Alice. "She'll never fall for a petition a second time," Jenna was saying. "Not your mother."

"You're right," Nora said, groaning. "She's so strict."

"Use Thad," said Sophie.

They all stopped talking and looked at her.

"Now that Thad has a car he'll drive, he can ask for a cell phone for his birthday," Sophie said. "They'll probably give it to him. If he gets a flat tire or something, they'll want him to be able to call."

"You're a genius, Sophie!" Nora cried.

It was such a shock that Sophie was tempted to ask Nora to repeat it.

"And if Thad gets a cell phone at sixteen," Nora was saying excitedly, "then I can talk them into giving me one at fourteen! Thad!" She jumped up and ran to the door. "We need you!"

"That means you might get one when you're eleven or twelve, Sophie," Jenna said. "Your parents will be totally worn down by then."

"You guys are so lucky, having older brothers and sisters," Alice said wistfully.

"What do you mean, Alice?" Jenna said, shoving Alice's shoulder so that she slid onto on the rug. "You get everything you want."

The babble of voices rose the minute Thad joined them. Sitting at her table, Sophie looked at her room as if seeing it for the first time.

It finally felt like hers. It looked like hers, too, with its painted window frames ("It's a good thing I *haven't* come in here in a while," Mrs. Hartley had sighed when she saw them), her brightly painted closet door, and her drawings tacked up in neat rows on one wall. She'd hung the piñata she made in the third grade in one corner and lined up her considerable collection of stuffed animals on the top shelf of her bookcase.

It was cluttered and colorful. Sophie loved it. She couldn't imagine how she'd ever felt it was empty. Why, the way it was now, it was downright crowded. If things kept up this way, she was going to have to put a VISITING HOURS sign on her door.

Of course, Nora would always be welcome to sleep here again if she didn't feel well. Sophie would just have to remind her to knock first.

∘ ABOUT THE AUTHOR ∘

Stephanie Greene has written many books for young readers, including the successful Owen Foote books and two previous novels about Sophie Hartley. She is the recipient of an MFA in Writing for Children and Young Adults from Vermont College.

Ms. Greene lives in Chapel Hill, North Carolina, and teaches courses in writing for children when she herself isn't busy writing.